AN OUTLAW'S HONOR

The CLAN MACLERIE Series:
Taming the Highlander
Surrender to the Highlander
Possessed by the Highlander
Taming The Highland Rogue
The Highlander's Stolen Touch
The Forbidden Highlander (novella)
At The Highlander's Mercy
The Highlander's Dangerous Temptation
Yield to The Highlander
The Highlander's Inconvenient Bride – crossover with A
Highland Feuding series!
Related stories (same clan 500 years later)
The Earl's Secret
Blame It On The Mistletoe in ONE CANDLELIT
CHRISTMAS

STAND-ALONE STORIES:
The Queen's Man
The Duchess's Next Husband
The Maid of Lorne
Kidnapping the Laird (short story)
What The Duchess Wants – for newsletter
subscribers only!
Upon A Misty Skye
Across A Windswept Isle
A Traitor's Heart in BRANDYWINE BRIDES
The Storyteller – A Ghosts of Culloden Moor (novella)
An Outlaw's Honor ~ A Midsummer Knights romance
Tempted by Her Viking Enemy
The Highlander's Substitute Wife (HIGHLAND
ALLIANCES series)

The KNIGHTS of BRITTANY Series:
A Night for Her Pleasure (short story)
The Conqueror's Lady
The Mercenary's Bride
His Enemy's Daughter

AN OUTLAW'S HONOR

A Midsummer Knights
Romance

USA TODAY BESTSELLING AUTHOR

An Outlaw's Honor

ISBN: 978-1-949425-02-4

Book Cover Design: Dar Albert of
WickedSmartDesigns.com

Print Formatting: Nina Pierce of Seaside Publications
Nina@NinaPierce.com

One

Edinburgh Castle
Scotland
Early March, In the Year of Our Lord 1193

Thomas of Kelso, though lately of the castle's best dungeon cell, moved his gaze from the door to the large rodent that sat in the corner opposite him and back to the door. Both of them waited on the same thing—the bucket of slops that would be brought in shortly. The rat had gained in boldness with each passing day, and now it no longer hid in the shadows. Its snout wrinkled and wiggled, clearly smelling the coming meal before Thomas even heard the guard's approach.

"Not this day," he whispered in warning to his competitor. "Not this day." Attempts to kill the vermin had been unsuccessful so far. Between Thomas's waning strength and the rat's speed and ability to escape through the small breaks in the stones, he knew the rat would survive him in this place.

The rat had learned to knock over the bucket once it was placed inside the cell, spilling its meager contents onto the putrid mess of the floor. Thomas was hungry enough to eat the scraps off the king's tables, but not off the disgusting mud and straw that lined this room. Though he might be desperate, he would not sink to that...not yet. Another few days without food? Well, he might do things a bit differently then.

When the door at the end of the corridor opened, Thomas crouched down, rocking on his feet to be ready. He remained in the opposite corner, away from the door, or the gaoler would not open it. He counted the steps, knowing it was but six paces to reach this cell. Pulling in a breath, he held it when the guard took that sixth stride that placed him outside the cell.

"Now, laddie, we will see which of us is the faster this day," he whispered to the rat.

Nodding his head at the creature, Thomas readied for the task. The rat began chattering then, as though in reply to his challenge. Or mayhap, the creature was just as hungry as he was. Thomas's long-empty stomach rumbled then, a reminder that the animal had beaten him the last three days. His dry mouth watered at the thought of any bit of sustenance he could grab, be it stale or rank or rancid. It mattered not, for Thomas must win this battle to live another day.

The guard stopped and slammed his gauntleted hand on the wooden door, the only warning Thomas would get to move away. More than once, he had not, and the guard made free with that gauntlet on Thomas each time. The rat now rose on its hind legs at the sound. The door swung open, revealing the guard there...the empty-handed guard. Thomas looked up from the guard's hands to his face.

"Put out yer hands," the guard ordered.

So attentive to the demands of his belly, Thomas never noticed the second guard until he held out his hands. The other one watched as cuffs were locked around Thomas's wrists, and he was tugged out of his cell by the short piece of chain connecting them. The scratching of the rat's claws on the stones in the corridor made Thomas look back.

"You lose, laddie," Thomas said before the guard slammed a fist against his head.

"Silence!" the guard yelled.

At that, he was grabbed by both guards and hastened along the hallway, up a steep flight of steps and into a large chamber. By then, his strength gone, the guards simply dragged him. When they went through a doorway, the brilliant light from the sun made him throw his hands up to block his eyes from the stabbing pain of it. The movement caught them unawares and they dropped him onto the ground at their feet.

Even that did little to slow their pace, for they half-carried him once more, relentlessly on to some place or person. Shame coursed through him at how low he had sunk in life. Once a mighty warrior, fierce and unwavering, to a traitorous criminal, left to starve to death in the king's dungeon. He had not even the strength to defeat a wily rat or to stand and walk to his fate like a man.

The only good thing now was that, if he were going to his end now, it would be quicker and less painful than starvation.

Their progress took them back inside, and Thomas could open his eyes. Drawing on his last reserves, he stumbled to his feet and walked the final steps to the door ahead. They paused while the guard knocked, this time politely, and waited for permission from someone within. Once granted, they brought him in and held him in their grasp before the man who stood there. The very image of power and wealth, this tall, muscular, red-haired nobleman arrayed in costly robes studied him for several moments in silence.

"*Brisbois?*" the man asked, staring first at the guards and then at him. One guard shoved a fist into his ribs.

"Aye." 'Twas all he could manage after that punch knocked the breath from him, and the question shocked him. No one had called him "Brisbois" since well, since his father yet lived. The legacy of his father's family who began as the royal torturers—bone breakers—when that first Norman king came to Scotland generations ago. Sucking in against the pain, he nodded. "We have been called that in the past."

"Leave us," the man ordered, dismissing the guards.

And they did, as though the hounds of hell nipped at their heels. Thomas faced the man who held such power and wondered if he was some minister or courtier of the king. Once the door closed, the man motioned to the corner of the room where Thomas now saw a table...laden with food. Bowls, plates, cups and more. His stomach cramped at the sight and worsened when the aromas of the fare reached him and overcame the stench of his own body.

"I have been told that the hospitality in my dungeon is somewhat lacking."

Holy Christ, this was...the king? King William. Of Scotland. The man his father had betrayed. The king.

Thomas delayed not, dropping to his knees and lowering his head. No matter that he was no longer knight or noble. No matter that he had sinned against this man and his kingdom. A man did not stand before the king of Scotland.

"Your Grace," he whispered.

"Rise, Thomas, and partake in the food there."

"Your Grace? I do not understand," he admitted, not lifting his head, and without moving from his knees.

"The table. The food. Eat."

"Aye, Your Grace," he said as he struggled to his feet.

It took only a moment, it seemed, to cross the chamber to the table. A single place had been set there, so he looked at the king before sitting. When the king did not deign to respond, Thomas accepted the invitation and indeed the order and filled the metal plate there with some of the roasted meat and bread and cheese. He counseled himself not to gorge, but his belly, aching with emptiness and need, controlled his actions.

All it took was those first few mouthfuls, barely chewed when they landed in his stomach, to begin the rebellion. Cramps spread through his gut as his body rejected the first good food he'd had in... a fortnight or two. Roiling and burning followed until he fell off the chair, heaving into the corner.

Bloody hell! Could his humiliation get any worse? Thomas wiped his mouth with the back of his sleeve and rested back on his heels, not daring to look over at the king. Only when a goblet was held out before him did he glance over his shoulder to see the king standing next to him, offering him the cup.

"Rinse your mouth," the king said. A hint of sympathy filled his tone, and he nodded to someone else. "Sit at the table."

Servants appeared where none had been and with quiet, effective actions, cleaned up the mess he'd made. They left without a word or glance at him. Now, when his stomach grumbled in hunger once more, in clear disregard for what had just happened, Thomas resisted its call. Another cup, this one filled with wine, appeared on the table before him.

"Dip a chunk of the bread's crust in this and chew it slowly."

The king playing serving maid to him? How could this be happening? Surely, he must be in that dungeon cell, having visions brought on by starvation and weeks and weeks in the dark and cold.

Thomas pushed his disheveled hair out of his face, and with trembling hands, he did as the king instructed. After the first bite and then another, the wine-soaked bread seemed to be tolerated. How long would the king stand idly by while his prisoner ate? Was this the last meal for him? Would the king declare his fate as calmly as he'd offered advice about eating while starving?

When he had devoured several pieces, Thomas swallowed a mouthful of the wine and then stood, facing the king.

"Your Grace."

"I have heard that you are undefeated in battle, whether on the field of war or honor. Is that true?" The king watched him with an intent stare even as he drank from his cup at ease.

"Though not of late," Thomas replied. Then he nodded. "Aye."

Once declared outlaw, Thomas had kept alive by moving around the country and continent, earning his way without a name by selling his sword to anyone who would pay in gold with no questions asked. Only when his prowess on the field became the talk of gossips and the court had his identity been discovered, and imprisonment on the orders of the Scottish king had followed. He'd not fought in months—his horse, his armor and his hard-won gold all taken on his arrest.

"I am in need of someone to carry out a task for me."

Thomas could not breathe. His chest refused to take in air. Hope swirled around him, and he struggled against the urge to seize it. He was a yet-walking-dead man, ordered to be executed at the king's pleasure and held starving in the dungeon while the king dealt with matters more important than a traitorous knight from a minor, though treasonous, family. Yet, the king's words inspired him.

Nay! He would not fall fool for a hint of something. For all he knew, the king was simply inflicting more pain and suffering on him before the final blow. Offering food to a starving man who would but die in another manner sooner was not kindness or benevolence. 'Twas cruelty, and well-deserved at that.

The king let out a loud breath and slammed his cup on the table. "I would have thought you would be pleased by the offer of a way to avoid sure death at the hands of my executioner, and instead face one that you might avoid by using your reputed skills on the field." In his confusion, Thomas searched for the correct words to say. He stood to his full height and nodded at the king.

"I serve at the pleasure of the king, Your Grace."

"That is what I hoped to hear, Thomas Brisbois of Kelso." The king walked to the door, and it opened for him. Attendants were listening to accommodate their king's needs without a word spoken. "See to his comfort." Servants poured into the chamber then, and the king turned to leave.

"Your Grace? The task?"

"At my pleasure, Thomas. At my pleasure."

The king walked from the chamber, and Thomas found himself in a whirling storm of well-trained servants following orders. It was days later when the king called Thomas before him to explain exactly what his task would be.

As the next weeks passed in preparation, Thomas wondered if death by the king's executioner would have indeed been easier.

Prudhoe Castle
Northumberland, England
Late in the month of May, in the year of Our Lord 1193

Annora watched as another messenger, this one wearing the livery of a noble house she did not recognize, arrived in the Great Hall and was escorted to the chamber where her father waited. Something strange was afoot, and Lord Robert de Umfraville was deep in the middle of it. This had been happening for weeks now, and yet her father had not spoken a word to her about it. Standing now and pacing before the huge hearth there, she wondered where the steward was.

"What is bothering you, child?" Her elderly aunt came to her side and took her hand. "Come, sit. I will ask them to bring some warmed wine to settle your spirits."

"Pray you to pardon me for disturbing your needlework, Aunt Eldrida." She patted her aunt's hand and led her back to her chair near the hearth. No matter that spring had arrived here in Northumberland, 'twas damp and cold inside the keep of Prudhoe Castle. "Here, remain nearer the heat."

There were times when her late mother's oldest sister seemed to lose her wits and her way, but once seated, Aunt Eldrida astonished Annora.

"I suspect your father is negotiating some sort of treaty or bargain that involves the king, or mayhap, his brother." Her aunt leaned closer to Annora and whispered then, "The ones who arrive without markings are usually from Prince John. He likes to hide what he does behind the king's back."

"Aunt Eldrida!" she said, drawing her aunt even nearer. "You must have a care not to say such things aloud. Especially when there are so many strangers coming and going." Annora trusted those few servants who saw to her needs, but not any of the others who worked in the household or visited.

Not in times like these that saw the king being held for ransom in foreign lands, and attempts to free him seemed to be the last thing on his brother, the prince's, mind. The nobles and merchants had been drawn into the battle between the Plantagenets for years, as the powerful dynasty fought amongst themselves for control of lands near and far. Her father had, as far as she'd been able to learn over the last two years since her mother's passing, supported the missing king.

And yet, with all these messengers lately, Annora wondered if he'd changed alliances.

Her aunt waved her hand at the remaining servants, sending them off. Eldrida of Northumberland had something to say and wanted no one to hear it.

Annora sat next to her and leaned in, waiting. Her hands were damp and left moisture where they rested on the front of her gown. This was not one of great value—'twas one she wore when seeing to the tasks of running the household—so a stain or mark would not be amiss.

"Have a care, Niece," Eldrida began. "Your father is

playing a dangerous game between the king and his brother. He proclaims loyalty to his liege lord Richard while giving support and more to John."

Annora suspected as much, for she'd heard that many nobles did the same. The king had been gone on Crusade for years and never seemed to have a care for his people here in England, except when he needed their gold. His brother was the same, but John, son of Henry Plantagenet and Annora's legendary namesake Eleanor of Aquitaine, divided his time and attention between the Plantagenet lands on the continent and their kingdom in England. Some thought too much time in England, but 'twas clear to anyone aware of the situation and the ebb and flow of support that he was looking to the future and consolidating his power now. No one spoke of it openly, for to do so would gain his attention and animosity, and both of those could be dangerous if not deadly.

"Your words of warning would be better spoken to my father, Aunt." Annora shrugged. "I am the one least able to heed your counsel. He cares little for me since I am neither a son to continue his claim here, nor am I the biddable daughter he demands."

"You can be used for his purposes, Annora. So, you have value to him. Your blood will continue his line. Your marriage will keep these lands in his family, under his control."

"But how, Aunt Eldrida? With no male heir..."

"The king decides the fate of the title and the lands," her aunt finished her words. "Or the man who holds his authority does. I would expect to hear news of arrangements for your betrothal, if not marriage, in the coming weeks."

As Annora realized the truth in her aunt's words and the enormity of the implications, a clatter rose near the entrance, drawing her and her aunt's attention. And the attention of everyone in the Great Hall, whether servant, visitor, or kin. Annora stood as a huge man entered.

He was at least a foot taller than most in the hall, who gaped at his every move. Reaching up, he lifted his helm from his head and pushed back the hood under it, exposing his lack of hair at once. Wearing a mail hauberk that reached down his long legs to his knees and heavy boots beneath it, his every step could be heard as he made his way towards the front of the hall, following one of her father's men. But he did not follow meekly. Nay, he surveyed everything and everyone there as he walked with the assurance of power in his stride. His gaze fell on her, and Annora could not help the gasp that escaped her.

'Twas not the polite expression of some supplicant knight. Nor was it respectful. After he directed a question to and received some answer from his escort, the man changed his path and walked to where she stood. Annora resisted the urge to seek cover. Her feet had backed her up towards the stone wall behind her before she realized it, and she knew how it would look to those observing this encounter. She crossed her arms over her chest and watched his approach.

"Know thy enemy," her aunt whispered, startling her. She'd not even noticed Eldrida at her side.

"Enemy, Aunt?"

"Well, a man like that is not your friend."

A shiver coursed through her body as he grew close enough for her to see that his eyes were brown. He was indeed more than a foot taller than even her and she was known to be tall for a woman. Gathering her wits about her, Annora watched him stride through those nearer her with the grace and manner of a predator. Though his gaze rested on her mostly, he never stopped studying the place, the people, the path and, she noticed, the ways out of the hall.

When he stopped before her, she lost the ability to think.

He was the most beautiful, most arrogant, most masculine person she'd ever seen. Annora stared at his face with its slight scruff of beard unshaven and its hard angles that made him terrifying in a male way. Her gaze moved down to take in the width of his shoulders, the massive size of his arms and thighs visible and intimidating under the chain mail and gambeson he wore.

He tucked his helm under his arm and smiled at her. 'Twas not a welcoming, warm smile. For a moment, she felt like his prey, waiting and holding her breath for him to make the first strike against her. Her body filled with an awareness she'd never felt before—parts of her ached, while other places tingled. She struggled to draw in a breath as the anticipation surrounded her like a vice.

The knight moved closer and leaned over to her, holding out his hand for hers. He wore no gauntlets or gloves; they lay tucked under his belt at his waist, and so his hands were revealed to be strong and as large as he was. Without thought, she offered her hand, and as he took it, Annora felt the callouses created by hard use rub against her palm. Lifting it higher and higher, he paused until she was forced now to look up to meet his eyes.

Hunger.

His gaze was hungry.

When he brought her hand to his lips in a gesture of greeting and honor, Annora could not be sure that he would not bite her. Another wave of aching, terror, want and anticipation filled her as he held her hand beneath his mouth for a moment without moving. Then, his brown gaze locked with her own, and he inhaled slowly before touching his lips to her skin. Scenting her as a predator did before the attack.

Without moving his gaze from hers, he opened his mouth and kissed her hand in a most inappropriate way. Insulting, really, for his mouth lingered too long, and his tongue touched her skin. The heat of him moved through her, overwhelming her in a way she could not describe. Then, he smiled.

A smile should soften one's expression. It should show pleasure or acceptance or happiness. It *should*.

This man's smile simply confirmed what she already knew about him—he was handsome, he was strong, and he was dangerous in a way she'd never encountered before. Yet, as he watched her in those few moments, she did not feel the fear that she should. Nay, she was certain he would not harm her. Instead, Annora thought he would simply consume her. He would take everything she had to give and want more. He would do things to her...

"My lord and the Earl of Northumberland await within, sir!"

His escort spoke in a loud enough voice to wake the dead or to interrupt this strange encounter. And yet, the man still held her hand close to his mouth, never releasing it and keeping it positioned so that she could feel his breath, his heated breath, on her flesh.

"My lady Annora, I fear I must tend to my duties. 'Twas a pleasure." He paused and kissed her hand once more. Before she could withdraw it, he turned her hand over and kissed the inside of her wrist.

"Sir!" Annora pulled her hand free at the scandalous, intimate action.

He laughed then, and, with a bow to her, he turned to follow the escort.

"Who are you?" she called out as he moved swiftly away from her now.

He'd heard her, for he stopped and faced her.

"I am called Thomas of Kelso, my lady. And who I am depends on many things. At the least, I am your enemy. At the best, I will be your..." When he would have said something more, the escort called him again, this time louder to gain his attention.

"Sir Thomas! Now!"

With those provocative words, he disappeared into the chamber where her father and his liege waited, adding to the mystery of the situation. The only things not a mystery to her were the danger of him and the threat he offered to her, body and soul.

Ignoring what he'd claimed, she prayed to the Almighty then that this man was simply a messenger. One who overstepped. One who insulted. One who was not part of her father's plans. That she would never see him again. He was too…much in too many ways. Annora was no fool, though, and she understood that a man like this one was not what she wanted him to be—a simple messenger. Nay, he was more a portent of doom and she feared for the poor soul that would be his target.

Suddenly, the door to the chamber where they discussed this matter swung open, and this Thomas of Kelso strode out, leaving a trail of angry voices behind him. Everyone in the hall scattered to avoid him now as his expression turned dark and menacing, and his hands clenched in fists as he strode towards the entryway of the keep. Her father charged from the solar then, only to be held within by his liege lord, the earl. When they slammed the door once more, she turned and watched Thomas of Kelso as he left.

Annora pulled away from her aunt, followed him out into the yard and watched as he mounted one of the largest horses she'd ever seen. Only when he began to ride away without a backwards glance, did she let out the breath she'd been holding in forever. She savored the relief of his exit for only a moment. As they rode through the gates, she caught sight of and recognized the standard flying over his party.

Dear God in Heaven, protect them!

The banners carried the symbol of the rampant lion, red on a yellow background.

He rode under the banner of the king of Scotland.

King William. King Richard. Prince John. All forceful. All dangerous. All relentless in their pursuits.

What in the name of heaven was her father doing? What kind of plans could involve the most powerful men in the world? She shivered then as the group rode through the gates. Her body trembled and shook, reacting now to what had happened and her fears of what was to come.

Somehow, Lady Annora of Prudhoe, daughter of Lord Robert de Umfraville and the late Lady Mildred of Northumbria, knew in her bones that she was in the middle of it. So, when the call came to travel to the west of England to a tournament of lords and knights and ladies from England, Ireland, Wales, Scotland and the continent, Annora realized the danger she faced.

With the backing of the Scottish king, Thomas of Kelso had challenged her father, and she was the prize. He was laying claim to her—body, soul, life and lands.

Gracious Hill, England
The Middle of June, in the year of Our Lord, 1193

The market abounded with people of all sorts, even now, days before Lord Yves's tournament was scheduled to begin. Though many merchants had set up tents nearer to the field where the main events, challenges, jousts and such would be held, the center of the town was busy as usual. Carts with all manner of foodstuffs—fresh from the summer fields or baked or cooked—lined the area. Roasting meat and fowl on spits and the honey-sweetened aroma of cakes and treats filled the air for blocks around. Those selling their wares were no fools—'twas those smells that drew customers.

Indeed, 'twas those that had drawn him there. Thomas's belly was not empty, so he should not be hungry, except that he always was now. Once he'd been granted a reprieve from the slow death of starvation or the quicker one of execution, all he seemed to do was eat.

Well, eat and fight.

Actually, his days were now filled with eating and fighting and fucking.

As a man deprived of all those things did when they were given back to him. Lucky thing for him, the king had provided enough gold to make certain he could have as much as he wanted. And, oh, he wanted.

Two months had passed since he'd walked out of that cell in the dungeon at Edinburgh Castle, and he'd not missed any chance to do those three things every time they were a possibility. Eating was the first thing he did with relish since his body was in no shape for the others for several weeks. When his strength returned, so did his need and want to bury himself in the softness that only a woman offered. So, he did, every night and most days since his freedom was granted.

Even now, walking through the market without the armor that marked him as a combatant in the coming tourney, Thomas noticed the glances thrown his way by the women there. His height drew their attention first, for since his youth, he had stood above most. His height had its advantages and challenges. 'Twas both in battle, when being able to see over attackers helped, and yet being clearly seen by enemies and the like did not.

When his appearance matured into a countenance that pleased women, he began to draw attention for that. He refused to be vain, but he accepted the truth of it.

As he bought three meat pies from one tent and two small cakes from another, he thought about the disadvantages of his looks and height when it came to women and could come up none. Neither his bed, nor cot, nor chamber or tent was ever empty of a willing woman or women.

Walking through the rest of the marketplace as he ate, Thomas took note of other knights and lords as they passed him by. By week's end, the fields and town and the Rose Citadel would be filled. There would be little open ground or places of privacy once everyone arrived. The cream of nobility and the dregs of the rest would be in attendance.

Right now, Thomas was more the latter than the former.

When the last crumbs of the cakes were consumed, Thomas made his way back through the town to the gate nearer the castle. The fields outside the castle would host the tournament, and that was where his tent, or rather the king of Scotland's tent, was located. Thomas would rather have remained unidentified until his private challenge of de Umfraville was called, but the king had other things in mind. Being a king, he did not deign to share all the important bits with Thomas. There was more, much more, to the king's reasoning about this entire endeavor that Thomas had not been told.

Oh, anyone who knew about the jostling that went on between the kingdoms of Scotland and England knew of William's anger over losing Northumberland to the English. He'd held the lands and titles until the present king's father had taken them away. Even William's attempts to capture them back as part of the Young King's uprising against the Old King had ended with him as a hostage in Normandy and paying a huge ransom for his release.

When that treaty was dissolved by the present king's need for gold for his crusade, William had still not been able to regain Northumberland or the title he craved, and Thomas only knew that Prudhoe and the de Umfraville family played some part in it all.

"Take the castle and the girl. I have plans for the castle, but the girl is yours," William had commanded.

Thomas's lands and title and wealth would be returned to him as a reward as well. The girl was a complication at best and a problem at worse. What did a man do with a highborn woman if marriage or fucking were not part of the bargain?

Oh, after his encounter with the lady Annora, he understood that he could swive her from morning till night and then until morning again. Her eyes were intense and intelligent—the aquamarine color of the water off the shores of a distant western isle he'd visited in his outlaw years. He'd never seen the like anywhere else in his travels, nor on another woman.

That mouth tempted him in his dreams. When she'd watched him lift her hand to his mouth and gasped, her lovely lips had formed the shape any man would want to feel on his cock—his flesh had hardened and waited for her attentions. That mouth would drive him mad. Her lush body would push him to the end of his control. The scent and taste of her skin, even that tiny sampling he took without permission or regard for manners or propriety, made him hunger in so many ways.

Even now, just remembering her face, the curves of her body and the way her curling blonde hair swayed around her hips as she moved, caused his cock to harden once more. He shifted his breeches and walked on, knowing with every step that the girl would be a problem.

Thomas strode through the gates, nodding to the guards as he passed. He'd arrived dressed in his armor to bring greetings to the Baron de la Rose from William, and the two guards standing here now had escorted him to the castle and their lord. Even without the accoutrements of battle, they recognized him now, and he knew the whispers would begin.

Brisbois. Bone-breaker.

By the time the tourney opened, there would be a list of challenges for him. The king told him to take any challenge he wished and to ignore any others, but that none of that should interfere with the fight William had machinated with de Umfraville's champion. Nothing should.

Thomas followed the road through the collection of buildings and cottages and such that lined the road to the gate. He found the path that led out to the area where tents were being assembled and places assigned by the baron's steward. Each day brought more and more people; the highest ranking of the nobles would be housed within the castle, while any others would remain in the camps. As the king's champion, Thomas had been granted a chamber inside, but the damp, enclosing walls of stone offered him no welcome. Nay. 'Twas better to be out in the open, under the stars, where he could breathe more freely.

"Eating again?"

Thomas glanced over to find the man William had sent there waiting and watching. Without hesitation, Thomas brushed any crumbs, present or non-existent from his cloak and tunic.

"Have you nothing better to do than wait and insult me, Martel? Is that what the king ordered you to do in my service?" Thomas passed by the man and entered the tent, ducking low to ensure he did not injure his head. "Has the Lord of Prudhoe arrived yet?"

"If you had accepted Lord Yves's invitation to stay within the keep, you would have been better apprised of those arriving and departing," Martel said in a flippant tone.

Thomas's first reaction was to strike the arrogant man for those words and the insult that dripped from each one. Sadly, Martel was not just Thomas's manservant and most times his squire—he was also the king's man. And he conferred with others sent by the king, whether servants or knights seeing to other "matters." 'Twas the duties Thomas did not know of that worried him the most. So, he flexed his fist and moved across the tent.

"Set someone up to watch. He must present his champion to the baron, and I would know who it is sooner rather than later."

"Aye, sir." Not so much mocking that time.

"Have challenges been made of me?"

"Only informal ones, sir. Most will come before the banquet."

"I wish to practice, so if some come to you inquiring, tell me. Or choose the best and set a time. If any Scots are among them, say aye." He'd seen several other Scots at the king's castle and understood that his was not the only play in this game. He'd rather train against countrymen than unidentified foreigners. Rolling his shoulders and stretching his neck, he knew he was almost back to his best condition physically. But staying with his training, or retraining, rituals would maintain his strength and agility now that he had reclaimed it.

The process of going from half-starved and half-dead to fighting strength had taken every day of these last months since he'd been freed from the king's dungeon. No expense was spared, no demand unmet as the convicted traitor became Sir Thomas Brisbois of Kelso once more.

As he searched through one of the trunks that held his clothing, Thomas understood that he was an instrument of the king, though one of retribution or of power or of kingly desire, he knew not. Yet…

Thomas only noticed the silence when Martel cleared his throat. Facing him, Thomas nodded.

"There is a rumor, sir." With his blank expression and amazing ability to give nothing away, Martel was the perfect, and perfectly aggravating, servant and keeper of secrets. A man more familiar with slinking about in the shadows than walking in the light.

Thomas crossed his arms over his chest and nodded once more. "Go on." From the way the man seemed to search for words, this *rumor* could not be good.

"Someone I know spoke to their friend who spoke to someone close to de Umfraville's stablemaster, who—"

"Bloody hell! Speak the name!" he yelled.

"Laurence le Govic."

Of all the names he'd expected or thought to hear, this one was not any of those. This name came from his own dark past. Never named but also involved in the conspiracy against the king of Scotland. Safely ensconced in the lands of his powerful father, a nobleman who counseled the French king, Laurence had not roused himself in years. Not since...

The food recently ingested rolled now in his gut at this news.

"So, 'tis true then?" Martel asked. "You lied to the king about never being defeated?"

Flashes of the fight surged in his memories. Laurence turned a playful practice bout into a full-fledged challenge. He claimed Thomas had insulted his father. He claimed many things—some true, some not. Even now, Thomas could taste the mouthful of dirt and feel both the broken jaw and the loss of face when he had to apologize to the lord. Fifteen years had passed, but those memories had not.

"I did not lie to the king," he forced out through clenched teeth. "I have never been defeated in tourney nor in battle. Neither has le Govic. Concern yourself not with that long-ago day and instead find out from your sources his past in the last five or so years. Find out when he arrives. Make yourself useful to your king and to me."

Thomas strode past the man and out into the field where tents now lay strewn like the acorns of autumn. Without purpose or aim, he walked and walked, weaving between those tents and the ones being erected in an ever-growing quilt across the green fields next to the castle walls. If any spoke to him, he knew not. He cared not. He stopped only when he reached the road that led to another gate into the village. Staring at nothing or no one, Thomas thought on the new twist to his situation and what he'd promised the king.

Laurence was a dirty fighter. He observed no rules, whether in life or battle. He won by deceit and cheating, by any means possible. He was relentless. He was skilled.

He was a beast when armed with lance and shield and sword. And now, he was a mature man with the experience of many battles. Unhorsing him would be difficult at best. Beating him with a sword would be nigh on impossible. Thomas needed another way to overcome le Govic.

Running his hands through his now-short hair as he stared at the endless line of travelers riding down the road towards Rose Citadel, Thomas began running possible battle strategies in his thoughts. Lost in those plans, he never saw her until the last moment.

Riding some distance behind her father, Annora was content to simply watch the countryside go by as they crossed what she'd been told were the last miles before reaching Rose Citadel. A name like that had her wondering if the castle would be surrounded by huge rose bushes grown high enough to be trees. As they neared the sea, a dearth of such flowering shrubs made her think that mayhap the castle had been named after a person—a daughter? A mother? A saint?

As the castle grew in size at their approach, peasants, merchants and soldiers gathered to watch them pass by. They reached the last curve in the road before the gate when a man who waited at the edge of the path met her gaze.

'Twas him.

Sir Thomas Brisbois.

A man called the Bone-breaker because of his history of doing that and doing that well. A shiver coursed through her body, reminding her of the danger he presented.

He wore no chain or armor of any kind now, just a well-worn tunic and breeches. No cloak surrounded those shoulders and their shape suffered not for the lack of armor or cushioning to fill them out. Due to his height, he could be seen clearly, even among others.

Annora met his gaze without faltering, though her heart raced, and her breath halted. Even without the trappings of destruction and war, he was stunning. No one could look at him and not know it. When one corner of his mouth rose in an enticing tease of a smile, she finally blinked. He smiled again, and a slight nod of his head acknowledged her.

Did he know how he affected her? Could he tell she was terrified? Nay, not terrified, but some other feeling she could not name now. What was worse was the way she reacted to him, Even now, she grew heated, and a trickle of perspiration made its way down her neck and spine in spite of the warmth of the summer's day.

"Good day to you, my lady," he said when she was close enough for her to hear his words. Oh, the expression in his eyes now, as they deepened in color and intensity, said he did indeed know what he did to her. "I hope your journey from Prudhoe was a pleasant one?"

Before she could reply, her name echoed along the train of travelers.

"Annora! To my side!" her father called.

Whether he'd noticed the knight there, she knew not. But it gave her the excuse she needed to remove herself from his close scrutiny. She touched her heels to the horse's side, and the animal responded.

"Good day, my lady Annora," the knight called again.

When she did not turn back to acknowledge him, his laughter—deep and masculine—followed her, and something inside her want to join him in that. A pull and push that had her wondering if she could or should or would ignore her father's call and answer this man's instead.

"Annora!"

Her name echoed in the air, and she urged her palfrey towards the front of those riding between her and her father. Yet, she could not resist the curiosity, nay need, to turn and look at him once more.

Annora had known only a small number of the men who guarded or served her sire or the other noblemen who visited him. She'd encountered some who had an interest in marrying her. She'd also had the chance to interact with farmers and merchants and traveling jongleurs and musicians. Never in her life had Annora crossed paths with anyone like this man. As moth to his flame, she wanted to learn more about him. No matter that she knew he was dangerous. No matter all the stern warnings to be mindful of her behavior on this journey. And, it mattered not that this man could be the very downfall of the de Umfraville family.

"Come," her father called, drawing her out of her risky thoughts. "You should be at my side to greet the baron. Pay heed to my words, Daughter. My very life could depend on this tournament and its outcome. Your future certainly does."

Alarm coursed through her, and the horse beneath her recognized it, becoming skittish and dancing a bit under her control. Annora tugged on the reins, and the horse settled.

But she did not. Could not.

"Father—"

"Not here, Annora," he whispered harshly under her breath. "When we are within and have privacy to speak. But not now."

His attention turned to some matter brought to him by his guard, and she glanced ahead at the looming castle before them. A wall enclosed the town and the castle, and Annora had seen nothing like it before. Baron de la Rose, Yves Le Strange, hosted this tournament, a scandal on its own due to the king's imprisonment across the sea and the turmoil throughout the kingdom. Knights and lords from all across England, from the continent, from Wales and Ireland in the west and from Scotland in the north, would be here to fight for prizes or answer challenges of honor before the highest in Richard's demesne. Titles would be won or lost. Marriages would be arranged. Lands would be at stake in the matches. Fortunes would be won or lost in the tourney and the melee to follow. And, from the whispers she'd heard, supporters of the king's brother John were gathering as well.

Interested more in the grand meals and gatherings than the fighting, Annora was certain she would never see the likes of this again in her life. Gossip spread amongst the groups of travelers they'd met along the roads about the king's brother and his part in this. And the Church's as well. All she knew about their situation was that a challenge had come from the king of Scotland. One that involved their lands and castle. One about which she comprehended little, while her father shared even less. Only her maid and others in the household had shared bits of what they'd heard spread through the servants.

So, she must find out the truth of what was to come, and how her father had been involved and earned the ire of the Scots king. Her father owed her that much.

Just before they reached the gates, a warrior in mail and helm on horseback met them. Though Annora recognized him not, he wore their colors of blue and gold, and the wolf and sword heraldry on his shield and surcoat and appeared ready for battle now.

"My lord," he called out. His voice was thunderous and alarming. "I have been awaiting your arrival." As he drew closer, he nodded to her. "Lady Annora, welcome to the town of Gracious Hill. Lord Yves awaits your arrival in the Rose Citadel."

With the livery he wore, he must be in service to her father, and yet he greeted them almost as one of the baron's men would have. Annora nodded politely as her father drew to a halt beside her.

"Annora, this is Laurence le Govic, our champion against..." He waved his hand to avoid saying the name.

"My lady." The knight held out his hand for hers, moving his horse close enough that their knees touched. Unable to refuse this gesture, she offered her hand, and he leaned closer still.

'Twas at the last moment before he bowed his head to touch his mouth to her hand that she saw it. Not the open expression of desire in Sir Thomas's gaze that made her want in return, but a naked lust that made her stomach tighten and her skin itch. The kiss bestowed was, thankfully, brief before her father called for them to move on. Rubbing her hand against the skirt of her gown, Annora could not ease the terrible feeling that now filled her.

As they rode on through the town, the knight spoke to her father and pointed out places of interest along their path. Once or twice, he spoke directly to her about a vendor who sold flowers and the best of the cloth and ribbons in Gracious Hill. All she could think about was that menacing threat in his eyes.

What had he been promised if he won the challenge? Could she be only the prize he received? At the end of this, would she be his?

His? She swallowed against her belly's urgent need to empty itself and tasted the bitter bile in her mouth. All she knew was the disturbing way she'd caught him staring at her, and it did her nerves and stomach no good to think on his intentions.

"Annora! Pay heed!"

She broke free from the frightening reverie and noticed that they now sat before the steps leading into the castle. Barking out orders, le Govic took control, and her father allowed it. After directing the other men, the servants and the carts carrying their clothing and supplies for their stay to different places, he walked to her side and reached up to assist her down.

"Here now, my lady," le Govic said, plucking her from the horse as though she weighed nothing, and placing her on her feet before him. Too close to him.

He held her there more than a respectable amount of time, his large hands encircling her waist and pulling her against him. When his thumbs crept up and caressed her breast, she pulled away. His strength prevented her from moving an inch.

"Sir!" she whispered. "Free me now." Annora did not wish to bring attention to this scandalous embrace, but she would not be accosted. When she tilted her head to look at his face, that terrifying look was staring back at her. "Sir!"

"You will be mine, Annora. And this will be yours," he said so that only she could hear. Worse, he tugged her hips closer until she could feel the hard ridge of flesh that he pressed against her. "All of it, my lady. All of it."

She drew in a shocked breath, ready to call for help, when he released her and bowed in what would appear to be a respectful gesture.

"May I escort you into the hall, my lady?" He hid behind polite language when others were watching.

Saying neither "aye" nor "nay," she rushed up the steps, moving away from him and towards her father. Reaching him on the landing in front of the doors, she took his arm. Though it should have comforted her, it did not. Indeed, the guarded and shuttered look he gave her spoke more than his words could.

He knew! Her father knew of this man's disrespectful actions. And he would do nothing to stop them.

She had been sold already, passed on to the winner of the challenge. She tugged his arm, slowing their progress through the entryway and into the hall filled with all manner of people now.

"Father, you would have me marry such a man as that? Truly?" she asked. When he would not meet her gaze, she had the answer. His reply, when they came, worsened the whole of it.

"He has just lost another wife in Normandy and has need of a new one."

"Another wife?" The words tumbled out of her. "How many has he had and lost?" she whispered, holding onto her fear and anger as best she could.

"You will be his fourth wife."

The truth hit her like a blow, forcing the very breath from her body. Wives of Laurence le Govic did not survive. From his rough, raw touch, she understood that in barely the time it took to inhale a breath.

She was being given to this man with no regard for her safety of life or limb. Little more than a bedwarmer or a broodmare if she survived his treatment before that. Annora had known all of her life of the little regard her father had of her. She'd comprehended in her early years that she was of less value than a prized son, who would have cleanly held onto their legacy and property. But the truth of it being spoken openly to her now stunned her into silence.

"Lord Robert de Umfraville of Prudhoe and his daughter, the lady Annora."

The loud voice of the baron's servant calling out their names at their arrival startled her, and she tripped up the first step that led to the dais. Her father took hold of her and guided her, and from the strength that he used, he must have believed she was trying to resist his plan. When they reached the place directly in front of the baron, she fell into a deep curtsy and remained there until her father lifted her to stand.

"Welcome to Rose Citadel, Lord Robert, Lady Annora," the baron said. When she finally lifted her head and met his eyes, she noted the serious mien about the man. Though she'd heard rumors that questioned his allegiance to the king or prince floated about, no one mentioned such a thing aloud in company.

Her father accepted his outstretched hand, and they chatted quietly, the topic she could not hear. Then she followed the baron's servant to a seat where she was offered all the amenities that a great house like this could. Only after she'd washed her hands in the bowl held out to her did she realize that both the baron and her father watched her.

Unfortunately, neither man's gaze gave her any hope of getting herself out of the future she faced regardless of which man won the challenge and which king or prince prevailed.

The high and mighty lords of the lands took their seats at the baron's table so that the opening feast might begin. Thomas had once more eschewed being placed as William the Lion's official representative, allowing one of the others who also kissed his royal arse to take the honor. He preferred being down at the lower tables, moving about, watching, studying and gathering knowledge about those attending, those fighting and those with grudges that would be brought to bear in the next week.

The coming days would be filled with individual jousts and fights to settle arguments and claims such as his. There would then follow on the final day of fights, a huge melee involving dozens, possibly more than a hundred, with prizes and honors going to the winner. Many a knight could earn great wealth in ransom taken that day. The long daylight of midsummer allowed even more time each day, so this would be one of the largest tournaments of the year.

Thomas walked the edge of the baron's Great Hall, greeting the few he knew, nodding to those who had challenged him and smiling at the maids or women who had already shared his pallet. It took him some time to find his quarry, but he did finally see her—not far from the dais, at her father's side at one of the tables in the front. Le Govic sat across them at the same table, and Thomas stood close enough that he could see the exchanges between his opponent and the lady.

One of the reasons Thomas had found such success in jousts and battles was his ability to read the truth in an opponent's face and body movements. He could see a feint coming before it happened—watching his adversary's eyes or the way their muscles readied. And right now, looking on Lady Annora as she sat there with her father and his designated champion, she was exposing all sorts of truths to him.

Fear was the most obvious one. In the way that her eyes flitted away when Laurence spoke to her and in the way that she held her body stiff and on-guard. Any shift by the man brought on a retreat from her, lifting her hands out of his reach or picking up something from her plate or her cup to drink. Only when le Govic moved back or repositioned his hands did she relax back towards the table.

Anger at her father rode clear on her face. Her lip curled in a mutinous response to his every word. Oh, she was careful that the man did not see it, for she turned away or eased the expression if he looked directly at her.

And yet neither of those stirred him to any response. A lady in her standing and heritage understood her place in the world—grow up in her father's household and control, travel to her husband's and live out her days in her son's. So, the fact that her fate was tied to something her father did or promised was the usual turn of things in a life like hers.

The lady Annora needed to accommodate whatever came her way, and the sooner she learned that, the easier her life would be.

Thomas leaned over those sitting near to where he stood and grabbed a piece of cheese and chunk of bread from the platter there. He would find a place to eat the whole of the meal, but for now, he grazed as he made his way around the hall...and observed the lady. Whatever it was about her that drew him to her every change in expression or of her body, he knew not. Still, he watched her and reveled in her attention and reactions in each of their encounters so far.

The king's orders commanded that the castle would be William's to dispose of, but this woman was to be Thomas's. The king, no doubt, believed he would take her to wife, for it was all but spoken as an order when the king's demands had been explained to Thomas.

But would he marry her? Should he keep her? Once his lands and titles were returned to him, he would be in need of a wife and sons. Why not her?

Getting bairns on her would be no hardship at all. Not with his hunger for the curves that lay beneath the oversized gowns she chose to wear. Not with her turquoise eyes and her mouth that would tempt a monk to sins of the flesh. He pushed those growing thoughts aside when her father and le Govic rose and left her there at the table alone. Her expressive face had not hidden her exasperation or bewilderment or her arousal when he'd teased her before.

Innocence—this was what it looked like. Lady Annora de Umfraville. 'Twas so long since he'd seen it embodied in a person that he'd almost forgotten its appearance.

So, why not her, indeed? There would be time for this decision after he won.

At first, as he turned his steps in her direction, devilment rode his shoulders as he considered how to bring that blush to her cheeks once more. After her father departed and before she'd noticed him, she closed her eyes for a brief moment, as though in prayer or contemplation. When she opened them, desolation filled her gaze, and it nearly took him to his knees.

Why it should matter, he knew not. She was just part of

the method by which he would regain all he'd lost in his life. She was nothing more than a pawn to be played, whether at her father's or his own direction. Nothing other than that was of import to his scheme.

The confusion and despair deepened the color of her eyes until they were a darker blue than the color of the sea. Much like shades of a storm did when passing over the depths of the ocean off Scotland and churning the colder, deeper waters to the surface. He stood in front of her for several seconds before she saw him, and he fought the reaction within him at her obvious distress. It took a mighty effort to bring back to mind the mischievous teasing he'd planned. Something in those first few seconds when she did realize she'd stared at him told him she could not accept any concern or pity at this moment.

Fragile. That was the word he sought to describe her now.

Fragile and easily broken.

Fragile and somehow, he played a part in it.

He slid into the chair opposite her and nodded. "My lady."

The lady confounded him in the next moments. She pulled herself back under control, the brittle expression replaced with one of politeness and distance. "Sir Thomas." Her voice cool and her face empty, she nodded at him. "Pray, join me."

Since he already had, Thomas took the words with a smile as the rebuke she'd intended. "My thanks, Lady Annora." He could play this game, too. "Where is your maid this evening? Should she not be at your side?"

"Thank you for your concern, sir. I was well-attended by my father and his...our champion until just now. My maid is on an errand at my request." She lied smoothly, for she did not know that Thomas had paid the young woman to slow her steps and wait for his signal to join her lady at table.

"Have her always at your side, lady. These tournaments bring in unsavory characters who have not the best intentions behind their actions and words."

"Do you speak of yourself, *Sir* Thomas?"

He could not restrain his reaction, and his laugh was loud and hearty. "'Tis possible, my lady. 'Tis certainly possible. So, you have heard my sordid tale then?" He would know what her father had told her. For some reason, he believed she would tell him the truth.

"A man who betrayed his king and country is now brought high and sent to represent that king in a matter of honor about which no one will speak. I only wonder what payment a traitor will receive if he upholds his king's honor?"

Cold and precise, her words cut through the rumors and innuendos to the heart of it.

"Did you not hear? I will win Prudhoe and its lady."

"I doubt your king will allow you to keep Prudhoe, sir. What do you get in this matter if God sees His way to favor your cause?" God, Thomas feared, had little to do with the battles and challenges to be fought in the coming week.

"If the Almighty concerned Himself with these small matters of insult and pride, what other greater matters would go untended while He dithered here in England?"

"Sir!" she gasped out in a whisper. "Have a care for such words!"

"Do you worry over my immortal soul, my lady? 'Tis already blackened and tarnished by many misdeeds and sins, so worry not."

She watched him with wide eyes now.

He reached out and covered her hand, there on the table. "But I thank you for your concern."

The touch lasted only moments before he removed his hand. She had not pulled away, only stared at the sight of his larger hand covering her smaller one. It was, he knew, far less scandalous than the kiss on the inside of her wrist he'd given her when they first met. And far, far less than he'd like to do to her, but that she had not pulled back pleased him in some deeper way. The lady looked away from his gaze for a second before meeting it again.

"I hope that you will receive more from your king if you win than just me. I fear you will be disappointed in your prize, then."

Thomas startled then at her self-deprecation. She was, he'd learned, accomplished at the many things a noblewoman should be and oversaw the household on her father's behalf. In spite of not having traveled far from her home, she rode well and was known to be kind to her servants and those who worked their lands. Indeed, she would be a worthy prize for most men seeking such.

Only as he prepared to say words that would express those thoughts did he stop. Nay, he must not make this a personal exchange. This was not about her beauty nor her accomplishments. Not about her noble birth or standing. And the king would not appreciate him sharing the details of their arrangement with their quarry.

This was about *him*. This was about getting *his* honor and *his* properties back from the duplicitous King of Scotland. She was only a part of the plan.

So, Thomas pushed off the soft feelings this woman engendered in his dark soul and laughed once more. Catching the eye of her waiting servant, he signaled for her to return.

"Ah! The missing lady's maid is returned to her mistress," he said, using the girl's presence to take his leave. "Be you more vigilant for your lady's safety and comfort, lass. There are bad men and dangerous things afoot at gatherings such as these."

His coin had assured her silence, so he did not worry that his scolding would loosen her tongue in this business between them. When he paid women, he paid them well.

"I do not need you to tell my maid her duties, Sir Thomas." The spirit was back in Lady Annora's eyes and in her voice.

Good. He much preferred that to the sad, empty temperament he'd witnessed earlier. He'd rather fight her than pity her. Their interactions were so much more fun when she was spitting fire.

"Indeed," he said, rising from his seat. "I will leave you in her hands then. My lady."

Thomas nodded and walked away as the maid whispered apologetic words, begging pardon for straying from her lady's side. Seeking out the shadows along the wall, he continued to watch the woman at the center of this undertaking. Though the king revealed little of his motives in seeking out this redress of honor, Thomas had heard some of the stories that bound William to those who'd held Prudhoe.

After losing his family claim to Northumberland to the English King Henry, William's attempts to take it back had failed miserably, resulting in him being defeated in battle and taken and held hostage across the channel. The ransom paid for William's return had added more insult to the matter. Yet, something in his instructions to Thomas spoke of a more personal betrayal or humiliation that involved the de Umfraville family. One that Thomas would help him remedy or, at the least, avenge its commission.

Lady Annora was, without doubt, in the middle of it. And though the king had promised her disposition to him if—when—he won, Thomas did not believe for a moment it would end that easily. Something more was at play here. Something powerful and unseen, hidden from him apurpose he suspected, pulled strings. The feeling in his gut told him that he was only one of the puppets.

Well, five more days, and it would be over for him. He would win his challenge against the lord of Prudhoe and his champion as he must, dispense with the girl and claim his lost title and lands. Five more days, and he would be restored. He would be known no longer as traitor and outlaw. Five more days.

And yet, it took only one day more to show him how wrong he was about this being a clear path to redemption.

After breaking their fast in the hall with all the other nobles and their host, Annora waited until her father and le Govic left for the field to seek out their tents and to prepare for the coming parade of knights. His warnings about staying to their chamber until he called for her rang in her ears even as she made plans to the contrary. In spite of her dire situation, she'd never visited a castle such as this or been in a place with this many people from such different places. The many inhabitants and visitors would be going to the field of honor to watch the opening ceremony, so it would be the best time to explore the town. She did not plan to waste this opportunity on a day that had turned out to be so fair.

With her maid at her heels, Annora made her way down from the tower where their chamber was to the main floor of the castle and then out into the yard. Gathering her bearings, she led Margaret towards the part of the village where she'd been told that the craftsmen and merchants sold their wares. Serving as chatelaine for her father's estate and working with his steward had given Annora an understanding of the goods and supplies that could be purchased in this distant place, which might be of interest to their own weavers and bakers and chandlers and such. In times of shortage or years of bad crops or unreliable sources, it was prudent to know of others.

That was the story she'd prepared for her father if he discovered that she'd disobeyed his command to remain within and work on her needlework or other tasks favored by ladies. Even now, as she approached the busiest and very crowded part of Gracious Hill, she thought it was a sound one. Following one narrow lane and then another, Annora stepped into the most amazing place she'd ever seen.

Oh, her own village had a marketplace filled with carts and tents and wagons offering a wide variety of foodstuffs and fabrics, butchered meats and fowl and the like. Yet, none of that had prepared her for the sheer size and bustle of this one. All she could do for the first several moments was stare.

Colors and sounds and noises and people! Coming to and going from the castle or the village. Talking in groups. Standing alone. Moving, always moving. Speaking in some languages she understood and some she did not—the tongues of the kings' courts and the common people. 'Twas simply astonishing to her that she was a witness to this!

Garments of every hue and sort. Ladies in fine raiment and veils of all colors, and knights and warriors in their finest armor and surcoats, heading out of the town to the fields for the parade. Banners floated on the breeze, declaring their allegiances. Peasants of all shapes and ages in serviceable garments of brown and gray. Tradesmen hawking their wares in loud voices, calling out the price of their goods and enticing anyone nearby to buy them. Others arguing and bickering over choices and costs. Bartering for items needed or wanted.

Annora could do nothing but smile and try to take it all

in. A glance at Margaret told her that the maid did not have the same reaction to the sheer scope of what they saw and heard there, just steps away from the safety of the castle. When she caught her eye, Margaret shook her head and motioned back the way they'd come.

"My lady, surely we should return." The maid reached out and took her hand. "This is what your noble father warned you about, my lady. I pray you, let us return to our chamber," the girl begged. "This is...too much."

"Exactly that," Annora answered. 'Twas too much, and it filled her with excitement and curiosity and need. "Stay here in the shelter of this doorway. I shall only be a short while."

Pulling out of the girl's grasp, Annora made her way towards the center of it all. Led by the aromas and the calls of the merchants urging people to examine their goods, she finally reached the main market area. Standing close to a shop that had its windows and doors thrown open in an invitation to potential customers, Annora was drawn by the scent of something sweet and spicy. Taking a coin from the purse tied inside her cloak, she bought a piece of the baker's special cake and began walking as she nibbled the edges of the honey-sweetened, sticky, gooey treat.

She'd stopped to ask about the location of the silversmiths, and where the coopers had their workshops, when the sounds changed. Glancing around, Annora noticed the shopkeepers and merchants becoming aware of it, too. As the ominous noise approached, one vendor and then another and another began securing their goods beneath carts and closing windows. Chaos spread, almost in a slow-moving wave, through the open area of the market from one side. Caught in the open there, Annora was too far from any of the shops to seek haven in them.

Turning this way and that, she sought a place that would keep her from being dragged into the wild brawl that expanded as she watched. How it had started mattered not now, only how to escape it. As a man was thrown to the ground at her feet by another who pounced on him, slinging his huge fists, Annora lost the ability to move. Then, a strong arm encircled her waist, lifting her from her feet and taking her out of the mayhem.

"Unhand me, you fiend!" she screamed. She made fists of her sticky fingers, ready to protect herself from his advances when she looked up and found..."Sir Thomas!"

"I told you of the dangers here, Annora," he growled at her. "Could you not heed my warning?" He never loosened his hold over her as he ducked punches, weaving through the mob and jumping over fallen bodies. "Bloody hell!" he yelled more than once.

Then, with an even more vulgar epithet, he released her and pushed her into a small alcove there. Turning his back to her, he fought off one man, and then one more, before grabbing her and pulling her along the dark lane, away from the fracas. Only when they reached a place where the noise and chaos had not followed did he stop. Pressing her against the stone wall, he protected her from others who'd wandered this way with his large body.

At first, his gaze was fierce and full of anger, and she held her breath for the outburst she was certain was coming. She released a ragged sigh as he stared. He panted then as she did from the exertion, but she suspected fury drove his, while fear fed hers. Before she could stop herself, she lifted her hand up and touched his face. Her hand looked small and inconsequential against the hard angles and rough stubble of a beard not shaven. He turned his head into her palm and inhaled deeply.

"Ah, you have visited Master Bartholomew's shop, have you not?" He covered her hand with his and lifted it closer, sniffing again. "His spice cake, covered in nuts and honey, I think." Her breathing hitched for a completely different reason now. "So much honey," he whispered. The tip of his tongue touched her fingers, where that honey still clung. "So sweet."

Meeting his gaze as he began to lick the remaining flavors off her fingers was the wrong thing to do. Terribly wrong. A huge error in judgment. His pupils flared, removing all color from his eyes, making them as black as night. He dawdled then, sucking her finger deep into his mouth and laving it with his tongue. Tendrils of need and heat pierced her to her core with each flick of that rough tongue.

She should resist. Pull away. Stop this madness. Fight him. And she would have if her body listened to her commands. Instead, her treacherous flesh pushed against him, surrendering her hand to his mouth as her hips pressed his.

"Is the other one as delicious, Annora?" he whispered.

From the way his mouth tasted and licked it, aye, he found it so. Annora melted in his embrace, as each slide of his tongue caused more tremors of heat to pulse within her. When every trace of honey was gone from her hands, she thought she might escape. She thought sanity and control would return. Then his gaze fixed on her mouth, and she was lost.

"Ah, your lips still glistening with honey. I would taste it there and know if it is sweeter than your own flavor."

Annora noticed, barely, that he paused a moment and looked directly at her. Almost as though he waited on her consent or refusal. Almost as though he would obey her if she objected. It mattered not, for her body urged her onto her toes to offer him access. He lifted both of her hands in one of his and held them over her head against the wall, imprisoning her there with nothing more than one touch. He slid his other hand behind her head and held her still.

"Annora."

Then his mouth took hers. Not a mere kiss. Not like anything she'd experienced before. He invaded, pressing his lips against hers until she understood he wanted her to open to him. And she did. His tongue moved within her mouth, seeking and touching hers, sweeping deep until she offered hers. Suckling it, he drew it into his mouth, and her body bucked against him, rubbing that ridge of flesh apparent through all the layers that separated them. When he released her hands, she clutched at his tunic, keeping him against her while he yet possessed her mouth.

She ached.

She wanted.

She needed.

The low moan that escaped her did not sound like any sound she had ever made before, yet it seemed to encourage him. He slid his now-freed hand over her body, gliding over her breasts, pausing there to caress her until she could do nothing but moan again and arch into his hold. Annora could feel his smile even while he kissed her. Then, his hand caressed down, over her hips and behind her, cupping her bottom and holding her more firmly against him. She spread her legs in answer to the pressure of his hand, and he moved her closer still, rubbing his hardness against her now.

Heat poured off of him. His relentless kisses did not stop, even when she leaned her head back to take a breath. His mouth traced down, near her ear and onto her neck, suckling and nipping as he went. At her gasps, he brought his mouth back to hers, drinking in the sounds she made.

If this was passion, she now understood the temptation of it. She understood how the weak fell into the sin of it. For, in this moment, she wanted nothing more than to fall with this man. Nothing mattered more than his touch, his mouth, his tongue on her, in her, taking her.

He stilled then, and she opened eyes she had not

realized she'd closed to meet his gaze. Now, a single sound interrupted this madness of desire—one long, loud blast of a horn echoed down the lanes, alleys and streets from the castle itself.

"The baron's men and those charged to keep the peace are coming to clear the streets."

He stepped back slowly, allowing her to disentangle her body from his. Her legs wobbled a bit when she stood free of him, and her skin felt on fire now. Her breasts swelled against the strictures of her gown and shift, and the tips of them felt abraded by the fabric. Could he tell? Did he know? One glance at his face gave her the answer.

Aye. He knew. The rogue knew, and from the smile that broke on his face, he was pleased that he could so easily draw her into such misbehavior. And that she'd exposed such a weakness to him so plainly

Annora straightened her cloak to cover herself and waited for his taunt. He'd played her. He knew she was inexperienced, and he'd used it against her. Would he tell her father, or worse, tell le Govic? Men used such things to make their opponents lose concentration during a fight. Whether truth or not, they would fling insults and innuendos at each other until something worked. Would these last moments of wanton behavior come back to haunt her? One look at that expression on his wicked face, and she knew he would.

"I think, sir, that you are more dangerous to me than any I might encounter in the marketplace you warned me of," she whispered.

He stared at her with those intense, dark eyes, and for once, he did not smile. When he lifted his hand, she startled at its approach. He smoothed her hair back, away from her face, and adjusted her cloak before nodding ever so slightly. "You have lost your veil."

That was not what she expected him to say. Somehow,

in the confusion of running to escape the coming mob, her veil must have come loose. If she made it back to her chambers, she could fix her hair and replace the veil before her father noticed. Mayhap Margaret...

"Margaret!" She grabbed his hand then. "I left her alone. I pray you find her!"

"In the marketplace? Where?" He ran his hands over his head, and she could imagine him doing that when his hair was longer.

"Nay, before we entered the marketplace. Near the entrance to the castle."

"Come this way," he said, taking her hand and urging her to keep up with his long, swift paces. It took little time to reach the castle's entryway, though 'twas not the way she'd gone. Sure enough, there stood Margaret; horror etched on her face as she searched the crowds for her.

"Oh, my lady!" she called out as Annora approached her. "I thought you would be dead. Or maimed. Or...worse!" she whispered.

"I am well, Margaret. Thanks to the efforts of Sir Thomas."

"Sir Thomas helped you, my lady?"

Annora turned to thank him for, in spite of his inappropriate kisses and sinful caresses, the man had saved her from being trampled by the mob or worse. He was gone. Standing on her toes, she searched but could not find him, even though his height should have made him visible above the rest.

"Come, Margaret. I need to return to my chamber. Remember, my father need not know of this excursion. 'Twould be better for both of us, I think."

The girl fell silent but followed Annora up the road towards the castle gate. Annora took one final look back and saw Thomas then. Just as she began to offer a smile and nod, hoping he understood her gratitude for his protection, he held up her veil and pressed it to his face as though smelling it. The knave! Annora clenched her jaws so as not to scream when his laughter reached her. She did stamp her feet, but it did not bring her satisfaction.

Turning back to Margaret, she made her way to her chambers and spent the rest of the afternoon trying to calm her heart and thoughts after the events in the marketplace. Her father never summoned her to watch the parade of knights that would open the tournament and she was glad of it. With so many attending the first of five days of jousts and challenges over on the tournament fields, she begged off supper in the hall and ate in her room with only Margaret. Through the quiet moments of that day, Thomas of Kelso occupied her thoughts.

He seemed to get the best out of each of their encounters, and it infuriated her. She'd never had to deal with a man like this—part nobleman, part outlaw, part unshackled from proper behavior and part unencumbered by morals. This was the man who, God willing or not, might win control of her. How could she protect herself against someone like him? In some ways, he was more dangerous and less predictable than the lust-driven le Govic. Her father's champion wanted to swive her and might tire of her when there was no sport in it. But she sensed that this Thomas of Kelso wanted more than her body. He wanted, nay he hungered, for more than he deserved and more than he should gain. He wanted more than what his king offered him.

More.

Well, the only way to hold her own against him was to learn about him and use that against him as he used her ignorance, her innocence, against her. She would seek out what she could about him, and she would be able to resist the way he undid her control. The way he tempted her to forget herself and be a wanton woman for his pleasure. If he were to control her future, she needed to figure out a way to control *him.*

When word came that her father would remain at the camp instead of returning to the castle, Annora decided it was time to seek out the secrets of this man who might be her lord...and master.

 Seven

The baron's men had cleared the streets of the brawl by the time Thomas made his way back towards the marketplace in the center of the village. The damage was much less than such a mob could have caused, and Thomas found a few broken carts, some tents torn down and a dozen or more men nursing bruises and broken noses.

It took little in a gathering such as this one to light the flames, turning a spark of indignation or insult into a bonfire. The baron's scrutiny and practice of having his men placed around the village and fields to respond quickly prevented this one from getting carried away. He grimaced as he remembered another place and time when it had. The price had been paid by those least able to afford it—the villeins and peasants who lived there and the farmers whose fields had burned. The wealthy man's son who'd taunted an opponent into throwing the first blow, and then stirred those watching into joining in the fray. The fight had spread and crossed the road from tourney grounds to the nearby farms. Havoc traveled quickly and widely that day, and a number lost their lives, and many their livelihoods.

All but the wealthy man's son, who was the cause of it.

Laurence le Govic.

Witnessing that had soured their friendship and eventually led to the fight that Thomas had lost. And his own disgrace. An uneasy feeling settled within him now. To have both of them in the same place with the same circumstances around them made his gut tighten. Pray God, nothing like that happened during this tournament.

Turning down a narrow lane, he counted the shops and looked for the alley he needed to find. Thomas hoped the man had waited for him. The delay was unavoidable once he'd seen Annora in the path of the growing mob. He had to protect her and get her to safety. Even now, as he approached the eighth ramshackle shop on the right, he tried to convince himself that it was all about allowing nothing to interfere with his challenge.

He turned into the dark alley and walked to the second doorway. His soft knock brought a reaction within, and the shuffling feet soon reached the door. A crack appeared as the door was eased open and then a familiar smile emerged.

"I had almost given up on ye, laddie."

Not many could call him "laddie" and live to tell. But then not many had known him as long as Iain Dubh had. As the old man pulled him into a rough hug, the urge to hang onto this man as he had so many times in boyhood filled him. Iain, his father's stablemaster, had fled during the troubled times for south of the border and away from the constant battles for control over the lands there.

"I had things to see to, old man," he replied, stepping away and nodding to the much younger woman who sat sewing by the fire. "Good day to you."

"This is my wife, Gytha." Thomas nodded once again at the young—very young—woman. So, the old man had found happiness here, after such misery in Kelso. Good for him.

"Iain, can we speak?" Thomas asked. He needed to be over on the fields, preparing for the two challenges he'd received and accepted. Martel would soon send out to find him, and Thomas would rather not involve Iain now that he was settled here.

"John, my lord. I am called John here. And aye, we can." Gytha rose and took her sewing into an adjoining chamber. When the door closed, Thomas smiled.

"And I am not your lord, *John.*"

"Old habits, milord," Iain said, holding out a cup he'd filled. "Sit awhile."

The man had lived in the borders all his life and knew more about the comings and goings, risings and falls and turmoil there than any other man Thomas knew. If anyone could give him insight into the king's reasoning behind this challenge, Iain was the one. And he might know something about possible treachery on the part of Lord de Umfraville or his champion.

'Twould be hard enough to win a fair fight against le Govic, but if the scales were heavy on the Norman's side, 'twould be nigh impossible. Thomas was no one's fool, least of all his own, so he understood what he faced more than most. He needed to find some weakness of le Govic's and exploit it.

After an hour's discussion, Thomas was not an inch closer to finding out the truth of William's challenge or a way to defeat his enemy. But Iain had given him one bit of knowledge about le Govic that he'd rather not have learned.

The man had lost his wife. He'd known that Laurence had married some cousin back on his father's lands after Thomas left for Scotland, but he'd had no knowledge of her death or the other two who'd followed her. According to Iai…John, his first and then second *and* third wives had met early deaths. Suspicious deaths, it was rumored. Violent deaths. Worse, though never accused because of his father's power and connections, all three deaths seemed linked to Le Govic's tendencies to use his fists against anyone who opposed or questioned him. So, this time he'd agreed to fight for gold...and another wife.

That Robert de Umfraville would willingly offer her as a prize knowing how le Govic's wives met their untimely end appalled even him. What could be behind this devil's bargain?

The thing that bothered him most was that it was Annora, an easily riled innocent filled with passion waiting to be roused, who would be given into such an arrangement. Truly, it made his stomach twist. Before this began, he cared not for he knew her not.

Now...now he knew her, and he wanted her. He would ignore, for now, the call of his long-dormant conscience about the terrible fate that faced her as his opponent's wife.

"My lor ...er ...Thomas, sir," John called after him softly as he walked away from the doorway. "Ye dropped this, lad." A piece of fabric, gauzy, silky fabric meant to cover a woman's hair, lay there in the old man's hand.

Annora's veil. The forfeit she'd not realized at the time that she'd lost to him. As he reached for it, John smiled at him and shook his head. "A woman, then, is it?"

He ran his hands over his head before reaching out for it.

"Is it not always about a woman, my friend?" He took the veil, gathered it in his fist and shoved it inside his boot. "Is it not always a woman?"

John slapped him hard on the back and, with a chuckle, returned inside where his own wife awaited.

Before heading out of the town to his tent in the camp, Thomas retrieved the veil and brought it to his nose, inhaling the last bit of the gentle scent remaining within it as he stuffed it back inside his tunic. Annora's scent. All he could remember at this moment was the taste of honey as he suckled and kissed it from her fingers and her mouth. And the sounds of her gasps and the quiet moans that escaped her at his caresses.

Her breasts and hips had pressed against his body, urging him to take her. Innocent that she was, had she even understood the invitation she offered him? When she should have fought him or resisted, instead, she'd opened and accepted his tongue, his mouth, his hands, even his cock against her. The feel of her soft skin as he plundered his way down her neck had caused his own flesh to harden and rise. Her firm arse had fit well in his hand as he'd lifted her more firmly against his shaft.

But for her shift and gowns, he would have taken her there against the wall in the shadows. The excitement of the danger of the mob had given way to arousal and need of the fleshly kind, and his body had been ready. Hers was, as well, even if she had not realized it. When he held her hands above her head, her breasts lifted as though an offering to a hungry man. He'd wanted to untie her gown and bury his face against them, licking the place between them and sucking those ripe nipples until she screamed.

Oh, aye, she would be the kind of lover who screamed out her pleasure.

Thomas stumbled then and realized he'd been so caught up in the sweet memories of the encounter with Annora that he'd not been watching his path. Luckily, the man he'd hit took no offense and just stood aside for him.

God in heaven! How was he to concentrate on the coming challenges when a few minutes of kissing and petting affected him like this? As he made his way along the road towards his tent, Thomas knew he could not allow the lady to be this kind of distraction from his purpose. He must put those thoughts aside.

When she was his...

If he won...

He growled aloud then, losing the battle to keep thoughts of her out of his mind. He was no better than le Govic if all he wanted her for were her sexual favors, whether in marriage or without. Asking her consent or not did not change it. He walked the lane of tents there and found his. Martel stood beside the opening with his weasel-like face tightened in anger as Thomas approached.

"You are late," he said as he held the flap aside to let Thomas enter. "You do not seem to be taking this seriously, sir."

"Is my horse ready? My squire? What is his name?" he barked out.

"Geoffrey," Martel replied in an even, unworried tone.

"Well then, where is Geoffrey? I have not seen him lately. Is he prepared for the morrow? My sword and lance sharpened? My chain sanded and oiled?"

Martel's gaze narrowed at each question.

"Well, Martel? Have you carried out your duties to me?"

Anger, nay frustration, pushed the words out. He did not wish his fury unleashed on the innocent squire assigned to him under Martel's direction and yet he lost control then. His body wanted to explode. Wrong or right, he wanted Annora. He hungered for the taste of her skin, for the taste of her mouth and her core, for the sound of her screams as he filled her with his cock. He needed...

"Have a woman waiting for me this night, Martel." There. He would take his ease and satisfy this need and be better able to focus on the tasks ahead of him.

"Am I a whoremonger now?" Martel asked.

In two paces, Thomas crossed the tent and grabbed the infuriating man by his tunic, pulling him up until only his toes touched the ground, and their faces were inches apart.

"I did not say she had to be a whore, Martel. Whether I pay her matters not to me. Young or old, slender or well-endowed and cushioned, be she red or black or brown-haired, none of that is of consequence. *Willing and wanting* is all I require." He shook the man a few times then, seeing the ire in his gaze at the insult. "And, aye, you are whatever I need you to be by order of the king." Thomas waited for a sign of acquiescence before releasing the man. "I will be at the practice yards."

He shoved the man off and watched as he stumbled across the tent. Gathering up his working sword and staff and leaving his cloak there, Thomas strode out and towards the practice yards. A few hours of work would take the burning edge off his need. 'Twas better to enjoy a woman's softness when the urge to plow was not so strong.

Some of the fighting had begun this day, with more to follow on each until the week's end when the grand melee would happen. Grand? 'Twas nothing grand about sliding around in the mud, slickened by your opponents' blood and sometimes guts.

There were few, if any, rules for the melee and, in spite of the use of blunted weapons, many men were injured— sometimes killed. Not intentionally, certainly not, but dead, nonetheless. A suspicious or cynical man would think it a good time to rid himself of a pesky enemy and 'twould be easy enough to mask under the guise of rough sport rather than intentional murder. Thomas walked to the fence that surrounded the practice yard for hand-to-hand fighting and watched as several men worked.

None were those he would face, but he enjoyed watching the techniques of skilled fighters. He preferred the sword and staff, as the two closest to him used, so he spent some time observing their moves. He recognized one man, having seen him at the king's castle during Thomas's own stay there—Sir Giric, a nephew, he thought, of the queen. He appeared to be the more skillful, but his opponent held his ground and fought back with enthusiasm. When they finished, Thomas asked Giric to practice with him and spent the next few hours regretting that. And yet not, for working strenuously brought his mind to the task ahead, and his body gained more strength from it.

'Twas not his choice to fight at less than his best condition. Previous tournaments had seen him at his peak—stronger, younger, ready to take on any and all challengers. But the last few years, and especially the last half-year, had worn heavy on him. Regaining weight and strength after the months of deprivation of the king's dungeon had not been easy to accomplish. Lifting his arms over his head, Thomas stretched out the soreness in his back and shoulders.

On the morrow, he would practice with his horse. The king's gift to his champion, this one was strong and full of heart, and Thomas was excited to be riding the huge destrier in the coming challenges. Whether or not he would be permitted to keep the beautiful beast was another matter and rested on the whims of the king...and the outcome of the coming battle.

Though the sun set very late near midsummer, and so the fighting and merriment would continue long into the short night, Thomas sought his tent. Martel had better have food and drink ready for him. Passing the last lane before the one where his tent sat, Thomas wondered about his other request or, rather, demand. Now, loosened up from practice, he would appreciate the attentions of a woman to ease him into rest.

As he reached the tent, a flash of regret passed through him. Even before seeing if a woman did indeed wait for him within, disappointment that it would not be *her* filled him.

So much for working Annora out of his thoughts.

Thomas lifted the flap out of his way and entered.

Eight

Her luck had held out, and Annora offered up a silent prayer to the Almighty in thanks for that. With it being one of the longest days of the year, she had plenty of time to visit the camp and find out more about Sir Thomas Brisbois of Kelso, who challenged on behalf of the Scottish king.

The first thing she learned was that he was not a boastful man with toadies around him to feed his vanity. Not about his prowess on the field nor about his handsome appearance nor, as it turned out, the number of women he'd entertained since his arrival here in Gracious Hill.

Of those things, the last one irritated her. As she continued on her way, having learned the location of his tent, she considered the reason for that botheration and did not like the possibilities. When she'd asked a small gathering of serving women what they knew of him while they stood watching him work in the practice yard with another tall knight, she lost track of the sighs and fluttering eyelashes at the mention of his name and his every movement on the field. The comments offered then caused a blush she could feel to the tips of her ears. Yet, even with her limited experience in the pleasures of the flesh, Annora understood some of it. Her body reacted to the description of his kisses, and she could almost feel his mouth on her.

When he finished his bout, and both men left the field, she rushed away with hurried thanks and walked in the direction they'd given her, choosing a path different from the one he'd chosen. "'Tis the biggest tent there in that lane. Biggest," they'd said laughing. "Like him."

What did it matter if he sought the delights of the flesh with so many? She had no claim on him or his affections. Even if he won the challenge, she could not bring him to task for such behavior. Even if they married, she would have no say in his pursuits of pleasure.

Her feet stopped at that thought. Annora glanced around at the busy pathway and moved to the side. Married? Was that his plan? Never once had he mentioned that. She had no idea if he had a wife hidden somewhere in Scotland, waiting on his return.

Oh, le Govic had not hesitated to make his need for a fourth wife clear. She would face a life of serving his needs until he tired of her or killed her, as the servants gossiped that he had the first three. She wondered what those wives' sins had been to earn such grim punishments and offered up a quick prayer for their souls before whispering one for her own. A woman had few choices, and she had little in this bargain, this arrangement that her father had made. There was no doubt from the rumors that she would lose everything—her dignity, her body and soul. Her heart hurt when she thought of her father's complete disregard for her.

'Twas then that the thought struck her—mayhap she could make an arrangement with Sir Thomas. Mayhap, in exchange for gold or something else he wanted or needed, or some aid she could offer, he would allow her to be free of him? If he fought only for the return of his tarnished name, mayhap he had other plans for a woman to take as his wife? If he had one, mayhap she could convince him somehow to let her go?

Before she could offer him anything in exchange for his agreement to her plan, Annora truly needed to know what drove him to stand for the king. A king who had, she'd heard while listening in on her father's rantings, charged him with treason and tossed him a dungeon to die while waiting to be executed.

What would make a man in that situation change his loyalties and fight for that king's claim?

Raucous laughter drew her attention, and she turned to find le Govic, her father and some of his cronies just yards away from her, in a gathering of men...and a few of the sordid women who flocked to events like this to earn some coin. They came from the direction opposite of the tourney stands where the last jousts were finishing. She tugged the hood of her cloak lower to cover her face and stepped into the shadows as they passed.

From the way le Govic shoved his hand down a voluptuous woman's gown, cupping her breasts while she rubbed her hand against his...his...flesh as they walked, she doubted he would make it to his tent. A moment later, the woman squealed loudly as her father's champion pulled her into the shadows near one tent, threw her to the ground there and tossed up her skirts. Annora looked away as the man unlaced his breeches and fell on the woman. Her father walked on with the others and left le Govic to his pleasure.

Like a pig rutting in the mud, he was.

And if he won, she would be the one beneath him, willing or not. To lie beneath him until she died from childbearing or from his brutal fists. Tremors shook her body as fear raced through her—the shudders tensed all her muscles and made it difficult to breathe. She looked at the path ahead of her and saw the large, well-appointed tent sponsored by Scotland's king, and walked faster then.

She must find a way to bargain with Thomas and must do what she could to make certain he won.

Slowing as she grew closer, Annora approached from the back and then the side of the large tent. Seeing a lamp's light escaping near the place where the tent's sides joined, she moved there as quietly as she could before peeking in.

At first, she could see little but the table and chair nearest the opening, the pallet in the corner and a collection of weapons near the back of the tent. Then, the soft moans caught her attention, and she leaned closer to see Thomas sitting on another chair nearer to the front of the tent. Until he lounged back in it, leaning his head against its cushioned back, she did not see the woman there, kneeling between his legs.

She was beautiful, fair of face with delicate features and, from the costliness of her gown and the jewels she yet wore, this was a wealthy woman. Whether a noble or the wife or daughter of a wealthy merchant or such, she could not tell, but Annora was glad that they only seemed to be talking.

The deep, rich rumble of laughter from him made her body catch fire. It was an echo of the sounds he'd made when he—when they—kissed in the alley. But instead of continuing to talk to the woman, he nodded his head and closed his eyes. Damn, but she was too far away to hear the words exchanged. She moved along the panel of canvas to the next opening, praying that her form threw no shadows that would reveal her. Pausing for a moment, Annora peered once more inside the tent.

Nothing could have prepared her for the sight before her eyes now. 'Twas not simply Thomas, sitting with a woman before him. 'Twas not simply Thomas, relaxing after a hard practice. Nay, he sat there, his laces untied, breeches open as the woman held his cock in her hands.

Annora swallowed once and then again and could not loosen the tightness in her throat and chest.

She'd felt him, that part of him, pressed against the most intimate part of her when he'd lifted her from her feet and held her to him. Now though, she saw that part of him—exposed, bold, erect, large—being caressed by this woman. Even the woman's two hands along it did not cover it from view. Close enough to hear their words, Annora now wished she'd not moved from the other place. The woman slid one hand down to touch and rub his ballocks, and he moaned through clenched teeth at her ministrations.

Annora could neither take a breath nor look away from the sight within. Every sound, every grunt or moan made the place between her legs grow wet, and caused a deepening ache within her. Then, when the woman leaned up and moved closer to him, Annora thought she might faint.

"May I, Sir Thomas?" the woman whispered as she licked her lower lip.

"Since you ask so prettily, Mistress," he said. He lifted his head to meet the woman's gaze and slid his hand into her lustrous blonde hair, loosening more of it from its braid. "Aye, Corliss. Take me."

Annora had witnessed many things that happened between men and women. Little could be hidden while living in a castle with a large number of servants and freemen. She'd seen couplings. She'd seen men taking women from behind like a stallion would take a mare. But never had she seen this kind of pleasuring. How would such a thing feel? To wrap her hands around the length and girth of his flesh and stroke it? To touch her tongue to it and lick it as he had licked the honey from her fingers? Something deep within her tightened as her breasts swelled, and she found herself aching to do just that.

At the first touch of the woman's tongue to his flesh, Annora stumbled back, not wanting to watch this intimate moment. She grabbed out for a handhold to keep herself from falling, and when she regained her balance, she looked up to meet the gaze—the angry and somehow amused gaze—of the knight within.

Thomas had heard someone passing by outside his tent, but when no interruption came, he ignored it. The lovely Corliss diverted his attentions well enough. The very young wife to one of the town's elderly cloth merchants, Corliss sought out the company of the male persuasion as she wished with the blessing, or benign inattention, of her husband.

She was lovely, truly lovely. When she knelt before him, her intentions clear, he tried to let his interest and flesh rise under her gentle touches and skilled techniques. And truth be told, for he would not lie even to himself, the interest was not there. After the innocent passion of Annora earlier, the experienced kisses of this long-ignored wife did not call to him.

Oh, she had finally been able to encourage his cock to rise and ready, but he'd closed his eyes and tried to imagine that it was Annora's heated breath on his flesh. That it was Annora's curling blonde hair that his fingers laced through as she approached. That it was Annora, and not Corliss, there seeking pleasure with him.

So, when he heard that soft gasp through the opening in the tent's panels, a gasp he recognized from this morn's encounter, Thomas knew she was the one watching. The thought of her seeing his cock erect and naked there, being handled right in front of her, excited him. Would she watch? Was she scandalized by seeing such a thing? Were her innocent sensibilities shocked?

Or, was she excited by what she saw? Did her body

soften and weep with arousal as she watched his flesh grow with each caress? Did she wonder how he would feel as much as he prayed she would touch him so?

When Corliss leaned forward, her pretty mouth open and ready to take him within and suckle him within an inch of his life, Thomas heard Annora stumble. Easing Corliss away, he strode to the opening between the flaps of the tent to see if she was still there, still watching.

And he met her shocked turquoise gaze there. A moment passed that seemed to last forever with their gazes locked, and he could read the desire there. She was a bold one, and there was not a shred of embarrassment or regret to be seen. Then, she was gone, and he heard her steps gathering speed alongside the tent.

Fuck me.

Whispering a few words of apology and dismissal to the draper's wife and tucking himself back in his breeches, Thomas followed Annora as she ran through the lanes of tents. He nearly lost her path several times, and then he did. Thomas turned down one and then another, seeking her without success. He slowed down and traced his path back to the last place he'd seen her. Then he stood and listened.

The sound floated to him from the dark shadows of a small hut there. Used by the baron's men to store needed supplies, it should be empty of people, and the door closed and locked. Instead, the door had been opened, and the noises from within told him it was in use. The sight of the silken veil caught on the edge of the doorway told him all he needed to know.

Without waiting, he tucked the fabric inside his tunic and then used all of his weight against the door, barging in quickly and with little sound. As he'd hoped, he interrupted without warning the people inside.

Le Govic had shoved Annora down over some of the crates and was doing his best to control her while getting her skirts out of his way. The edge of the door caught the man and knocked him to one side, allowing Annora to escape le Govic's grasp. As he reached out to grab her hair and pull her back, Thomas landed several blows on the man's jaw and then, aiming for his ribs, in his side. Annora managed to get nearer the door while Thomas blocked le Govic's path.

"You have no right to interfere here!" le Govic growled at Thomas. "She is mine!"

"Until the challenge is called and met, she is not," Thomas answered quietly. Though he could see Annora shivering there, he would not take his attention off le Govic. He knew better.

"Lord Robert gave me permission, you Scots bastard." Le Govic swiped the back of his hand across his face. "Said I could have her now since defeating you is a given. I am the only man to lay you low, and we both know it."

Thomas blew out heavy breaths, trying to ignore the insult and the temptation to finish the man here and now.

"Did the lady give you her permission?"

Le Govic just laughed at his question and did not reply. With her father's leave, le Govic could do as he wanted. Her virtue would matter not when this was all over, and one king or another triumphed. The man moved towards Annora. Thomas grabbed hold of his belt and used his opponent's own motion and Thomas's weight against him, managing to shove him out of the hut and into the lane. Blocking the door and her, he waited for the attack. He knew that le Govic would not give up so easily. Just as the knave clenched his hands into fists to strike out, a group of mounted knights rode down the lane there.

"The curfew is called! The gates are closing for the night!" the commander of the troop called out. Loud blasts from horns could be heard all across the fields.

The baron had made it known that order would be kept

on his lands during this tournament, and the appearance of these guards and the earlier quick response to the brawl in the marketplace spoke of his intention to see to that.

Though le Govic looked as if he would remain, the last man slowed as they passed and called out to him, "Lord de Umfraville seeks you, sir. At his tent."

Like a bitch brought to heel, le Govic turned and walked away without hesitation. So, 'twould seem that theirs was also an unholy alliance of some sort, with le Govic in thrall to the Lord of Prudhoe.

Once the area was cleared, Thomas walked to the hut and pushed the door open. Annora stood where and as he'd left her, in the dark corner of the shack, shivering. Now that the curfew was called, the gates would also be closing, and no one would enter or leave the castle until the morn. Annora was caught outside.

"Come, lass," he whispered. He tugged her cloak back into place and pulled the hood of it over her head and then down low to cover most of her face. "You must seek shelter for the night, and we will get you back inside as soon as the gates open in the morn."

"But, my father—" she began, even while allowing him to tie her cloak tightly. "He will..."

"No one will rouse early on the morrow. Far too much ale and wine has been imbibed this night. Unless le Govic reveals his own misdeed, your father will know nothing of this."

"But you—" she said. "Why are you not yelling at me?"

He had yelled at her the last time he found her in a dangerous situation, but he could see the fear in her gaze and feel it in her. He had not been in time to stop all his opponent's attentions. The lass had been terrified and nearly savaged by her father's man.

"I wish not to be detained by the baron's guards for breaking the peace, sweet. Come," he said, gathering her close. "My tent is over on the next lane."

Though she stiffened for a moment, she relented and allowed him to guide her. But he understood at least one of the reasons for her hesitation.

"Worry not. She is gone. And I give you my word that you will be safe there."

Soon, he held the flap open and allowed her to walk inside before tying the cords that would keep the flaps down. Now that he had her here, what in bloody hell was he to do with her? She stood still just where he left her at the entry while he sought a blanket and a cup of something stronger than ale to soothe her.

"Here now, sit here," he said, offering her the other chair that was positioned closer to the brazier.

He held the cup of wine fortified with a drop or two of the juice of the poppy up to her lips and tilted it until she swallowed some. Martel had made it up for Thomas to ease the pains and aches of the constant injuring and bruising left by hours of practice these last few months. He used it sparingly, but it would help the lady's distress right now.

Another sip and another, and soon the shivering eased a bit. He left the cup in her grasp as he tossed the blanket around her shoulders. Thomas stirred the burning embers to force them to give up a bit more heat. Midsummer or not, the air cooled quickly once the sun set, and a chill already filled the tent.

Turning to face her, he crouched down across from her and waited. After a few more sips emptied the cup, she held it out to him.

"Are you better now?"

She nodded.

"Did he hurt you?" He held his breath, believing he'd been in time. When she did not reply, he whispered again. "Did he hurt you, Annora?"

"Not in that way." Her slender hand moved to her neck.

"How so, then?"

His voice in that deep, soft, concerned tone worried her more than when he yelled or taunted her. Or when he laughed. She met his gaze then. Eyes the shade of the darkest trees met hers. She nearly forgot his question when he stared at her so.

"Where are you hurt, lass?" He stood then and moved closer. This time his gait was not that of a predator as his approach had been at their first encounter. Nay, this time, he resembled one coming closer to a terrified cornered creature that would bolt for freedom at any moment. Was she that?

"My neck is bruised, I fear," she said. Untying her cloak, she lifted one side of it. Without her veil in place and with most of her hair yet caught up in the braid that Margaret had crafted earlier, her neck was bare to him. Without a looking glass, she could not see the extent of it. "Is it badly injured?"

If she admitted the truth of how she felt, Annora would have to say that the wine he'd offered her had warmed her and eased whatever pain she might be feeling from the brutish grasp of le Govic. The dastard had grabbed her from behind and pulled her from the lane into that hovel, holding his other hand over her mouth so she could not scream.

He'd kicked the door loose and forced her inside. His strong fingers had dug into her shoulder and neck as he tried to force her to his will. She'd tried to scream and fight him off, but he was too strong. Too rough. She closed her eyes at that memory.

If Thomas had not come back...

If Thomas had not found her...

She dreaded the very thought of that brutality and knew in that moment what her life would be if her father's man won this challenge. So, Thomas's gentle touch on her shoulder startled her. She'd been so caught up in the memories of the attack that she'd not heard him.

"Aye, you will wear the mark of his hand there," he said. His soft tone now was not what she expected to hear as he lifted his fingers and walked away. The man came back with a cool cloth and, after easing her gown out of the way, he placed it on the worst of the injury. "I have some liniment I use when my horse is injured that would work on it, but I suspect you would be insulted by such a thing."

She laughed then, surprising herself and him. She noticed that the edges of his eyes crinkled, and the corners of his mouth lifted in the first genuine smile that she'd witnessed from him.

"I am quite horrified, sir, that you would offer something used on your horse to me." She was not completely serious or even a bit outraged by his words. His almost-kind offer made to see to her injury was unexpected.

"As my dear, departed lady mother would be if she heard me do so," he said as he crouched beside her once more. "Somehow, Lady Annora, you seemed more practical and less frivolous than other ladies to whom I speak. I but considered its *practical* uses and not its true purpose."

"But a horse liniment, Sir Thomas? Truly?"

"Mayhap I should have hidden its origin from you? Proclaimed it a wondrous cream for the skin from... France?"

She smiled then, relaxing for the first time since the attack. Or so she thought until her hands began shaking and she could not stop them.

"Here now, lass," he said as he moved closer. Tugging the ends of the blanket tighter around her, he began to rub her arms briskly. "Tis not an uncommon reaction to a battle."

"A battle?"

He drew her closer and held her in a warm embrace. She could smell the scent of him as she rested her head on his shoulder, allowing his soothing motion to continue.

"Aye. You faced down a dangerous opponent and walked away. This," he rubbed once again to ease the shivers that raced through her, "is your body's reaction to facing that danger."

"Has yours reacted like this?" Did men, knights, warriors, experience this, too, or was it just for weak women to endure?

"Nay, mine was nothing so tame as this. After my first battle, when I saw killing so close that I could smell it, I heaved my guts out in the grass. Several times. Loudly and in plain sight of my lord and his men." He laughed, and the sound of it rumbled through her as he held her. "I was not alone, for battle and death causes many brave people to crumble afterwards."

Annora sat quietly in his embrace then, letting his warmth and strength seep into her. For one moment, a brief one, she felt safer than she'd felt in so long. The tears fell before she could control them.

"Come here," he whispered. "'Tis over now." He slid her off the chair and onto his lap as he sat back on the floor there. "You are safe now."

"Unless I am discovered outside of my chamber. Unless my father learns I was here in the camp. Unless le Govic's attempts to have his way with me become common knowledge." She sighed then and whispered the one true danger she faced. "Unless le Govic wins."

"'Tis my turn to be insulted," Thomas said. "Not one of those included being held like this by the dangerous Sir Thomas of Kelso, called Brisbois as he is descended from the king's torturers. And one of the ablest knights to enter a field or battle."

His good humor eased many of her fears. In each encounter with him, he had tried to intimidate her, or to make advances, or to prove his attractiveness or prowess. Here, now, he was simply trying to make her feel better. She sat up and stared at him.

"Why are you being kind to me?" He looked away but not before she saw the confusion there deep in his gaze. "Why save me at all?" Annora pushed back to stand and removed the now-warm cloth from her neck. "Why did you leave Mistress...er...that woman to follow me?"

"The better question is, why were you spying on me? Standing outside my tent, disturbing my privacy?" he asked back without answering her questions.

He stood and crossed his arms over his chest and waited on her answer. If she was beginning to think clearly, the shock of that attack was easing. He was still furious enough to tear le Govic apart, but Thomas would have to direct that ire into their coming jousts. Now, he watched her stand tall and regain herself.

"I came here to discuss an arrangement with you."

Of all the things Thomas thought he would hear those words were not it. His body reacted in all sorts of inappropriate ways to the possible meanings of the word.

Tamping the rush of heat in his blood, he cleared his throat.

"What kind of arrangement?" he asked. Even he noticed the change in his voice as his body hoped it was right.

She glanced away for a moment and then back at him. The expression in those remarkable eyes changed from moment to moment, exposing a myriad of emotions to him.

Hope. Fear. Confusion. Temptation. Panic. Arousal.

One and then another flashing as she tried to control herself after making such an offer. She looked around the tent, staring for a long time at the pallet in the corner, before nodding in the other direction.

"May we sit?"

"Of course," he said, pulling the more distant chair closer to the other one and holding out his hand for her to take it. "Would you like some more wine?" She walked over to the one that had been farther away and chose that one. The urge to laugh as he recognized which chair she'd chosen nearly overwhelmed him. "Plain wine."

He poured some into two cups and brought them over. When he caught her glance examining his body from the belt down and then glancing at the chair, he knew she'd seen as much as he'd suspected. After handing her one cup, he pulled a stool over from near the table and used that instead. 'Twould be a cruel taunt if he sat in the one where Corliss had begun to pleasure him. Cruel to the innocent now across from him and cruel to himself for he would spend the entire time trying not to think on it.

"Tell me of this arrangement you seek." He took a long swallow of the wine and waited.

The lady tripped over words several times before finding the ones she sought. "First, pray tell me what you gain from your king if you win this challenge?" she asked. "Wealth? Prudhoe Castle? Me? Anything else?" The becoming blush that crept into her cheeks just then made him want to lean closer and feel that heat against his mouth. She shook her head then and changed the question. "Do you plan to marry me if you win?"

"That is bold, my lady. Is it not your place to watch and wait and accept the outcome as determined by your father and my king?"

"Is that what you are doing, Sir Thomas?" she asked. Tossing back the last wine in her cup, she stood and walked over to the table. The cup landed with a bit of a bang on the surface as she turned to face him.

"I ask in good faith, sir. Although I hear this and that about you, about the challenge, about my possible future, I would rather know what is coming then guess about it. I would rather prepare for it. Especially if..." She stopped then and looked at him. "I pray you, tell me what you gain."

Thomas hesitated, unsure he wanted to give her what she asked. Did she truly want this knowledge for her own use, or was she yet her father's pawn? She pressed on when he did not speak.

"Will he forgive your treason? Wipe the stain from your name and honor?" She was daring to confront him with that.

"I am no fool, lady. I would not hear his offer until that was accomplished." Not completely true, however, she did not need to know the details of the manner in which the deal was made. "Besides, how could I be here with that crime of treason being held against me? No truce would allow me that."

"Forgive me, sir, for my accusation." She entwined her fingers and held her hands before her. He wanted to reach out and ease the tension in them. When he thought she had softened in her approach, she straightened her shoulders and relaxed her hands. "So, you are now once more in his good graces. What else do you stand to gain by this when you yet risk so much?"

"Risk?"

"Life and limb. Reputation on the field. Horse. Armor. Gold?" She'd just reminded him in specific detail of everything he could lose, and all he wanted to do was take her and kiss her until she could no longer speak. "Pray tell me."

"The castle is the king's." He shrugged. "I know not why it is important to him, but it is. He is relentless in his desire to claim it." He drank the rest of his wine. "And you are to be mine."

"If all you receive as a prize is me, then you win little," she whispered. "Again, I ask you—do you plan to marry me if you are the victor of the challenge?"

She pushed him. Her words were as much a challenge as the official one made by his king to her father. Did she wish to marry him? A traitor, former or no. A man unworthy of trust. A man who would sell his very soul to the highest bidder. Or was this only to gain knowledge for her father's use?

His delay in answering did just that—for she nodded slightly, understanding he would not, and returned to sit in the chair, considering what this meant. Words to ease her concern, words to appease her, words to explain all sat on his tongue, urging him to let them loose. But Thomas had learned the danger in sharing too much the hardest way— by losing all he had and all those he loved. No matter that he liked her. No matter that he wanted her. No matter... He would not expose his reasons to her. Her words startled him then.

"So, you will seek a wife elsewhere if," his raised eyebrow stopped her then, "*when*, when you win. And since we know le Govic has *lost* every wife he has taken and now seeks another presumably for the same purposes, then the possibilities I face are to live as your leman or," she paused, "or when he tires of me, die as his wife."

Though it was the truth, it turned his stomach to be spoken of in such a plain manner as this, and that she equated him with le Govic. She knew of the fate of le Govic's wives back on his father's lands. How she'd learned such things, he did not ken, but she had. Le Govic was a clear danger to her life and limb while he himself was a threat to her virtue and honor and future.

Yet, was Thomas any better a choice? Even without a wife to claim yet, he did not plan to marry her. Oh, he wanted to have her, but as he'd come to realize in the last days as he'd prepared for his upcoming battle, marriage was not part of it. Marriage could not be.

After regaining his lands and titles, he needed a well-connected marriage to renew and expand his family in Scotland. Through his mother's claims and kinship to several powerful clans in the north, he could make an alliance that would see him return his family to its rightful place of honor. His sons would further that with their own marriages. All would be well again for the Brisbois family for generations to come.

For, if he won, there would be no dowry offered for Annora by her father or his family. No matter how much he might want her in his bed, marriage to her would not offer the necessary alliances or wealth to help his cause or to claim his heritage. No, he would not, could not offer marriage to her.

First, though, he must win before any of this could be considered.

"I would like to know that there is an ending to this that leaves me alive and well," she began, her voice gaining strength with each word, "So I offer myself to you." She let out a breath after those shocking words. "If I must suffer your attention, I will do so, but only until you marry elsewhere. Then I will leave."

He'd been ignorant of so many things in his life. He'd never realized his father had involved them in a traitorous plot against King William. He had not thought he would survive the imprisonment he'd suffered. And never in his wildest imaginings did he think to hear a lady such as Annora de Umfraville both offer herself to him and insult him in one small string of words.

He wanted to laugh aloud at her audacity. Then, he wanted to shout denials that she would never have to *suffer* his attentions. Mostly though, he wanted to cheer her for having the practical nature that she did. She stood there, not begging, but trying to bargain her way to a small measure of control where she had none. Most women never controlled their lives or fortunes. He owed her the honor of a reply.

"Are there other demands you would make, my lady?" he asked. "Now would be the time to speak of them."

"I pray you, do not mock me, sir!" she said through clenched jaws. "I am negotiating for my life and my honor."

"I do not, my lady. As I have recently been involved in making such an arrangement of my own, I wish all the conditions to be clear before any agreement is reached."

She let out a breath and took in another. "First, I would want this to remain between us. Let them believe we are to marry until after we leave this tourney," she said slowly without meeting his eyes. "I would prefer to finish this with my dignity intact." Then, raising her gaze to his, Annora looked at him and waited for his assent.

"I do not intend to humiliate you, my lady. No one here need know of our arrangement if we come to one," he said softly. And, in truth, he had not intended such a thing. Once the deed was done, he would return to Scotland and the king swiftly for the restoration of his titles and more, and he would think about the rest once that was done.

"There are a few other items to discuss then. I would

like a small settlement when 'tis over and done. I expect my belongings to be mine and to go with me when I leave. And—" She did not finish this last one. Her gaze left his and stared at something over his shoulder.

"And? Come now, lady, do not lose courage now, for you are bargaining like the boldest merchant I have seen in my life. Aye, the fishmonger at Gracious Hill's docks cannot claim to be superior to your skills. If you please, your next requirement?" Thomas was enjoying this too much. To hear such a woman speak so plainly, and all the while exposing more to him than she realized, was something he'd never experienced.

"And I would want you to take no others to your bed while you...while I am...during...this arrangement."

Annora continued to amaze and even shock him with every word she spoke. Her face was now the fiery red color of last evening's sunset.

"Do you understand what that means, Annora?" He crossed his arms over his chest and leaned back, enough to emulate his earlier position in the chair but not enough to fall off.

"Aye," she said. Then her white teeth worried the edge of her lower lip, and she shook her head. "Nay, in truth, I do not," she whispered.

"It means that I will have only *you,* but I will *have* you. I will have you any time, any place and in any manner I desire. And as many times as I want." He stepped closer, lowering his voice. "I could marry days after the tournament, if a suitable wife is found when my title and lands are returned by the king, or it could take years. Either way, you will be mine to satisfy my needs." He took her shoulders and drew her in. "Mine and mine alone."

His body raged at him to make that *having* happen now, right now, right here. Struggle for control he must, for Thomas would not give in. Was he trying to frighten her? Aye. She must consider the cost she would incur if he agreed. Would she ever suffer at his hands? Nay. Neither would he hold back once she was his. Though it rubbed him harshly that she was viewing life in his arms and in his bed as terrible a fate as one as le Govic's wife would be, he was filled with a sense of...pride?...as she made her case to him.

So far, though, she had not mentioned what she would actually offer as part of this bargain, for all the rest was already in his control. Leaning down until their mouths were a scant inch apart, he whispered, "And what do you offer in return, if I accept and I win?"

His direct words coming during such a candid conversation should have been expected, and yet there were not. She drew back as far as his hold would allow. Instead of panic or indecision, she was calm and her gaze clear as she now met his.

"My offer to you is this," she said. "I will come willingly to your bed—"

"A given," he replied. A lie he knew, but it mattered not. "Any time, any place, in whatever manner I wish?"

"Aye."

She swallowed then, trying to make the words come out of her dry, frightened mouth. His body was hot and hard against her as she tried to think about what his words meant. His hands held her close but did not hurt or frighten her. Nay, 'twas not his body that did that. 'Twas the intensity of his desire that filled his every word and glance.

"Truly?"

Did he wish to bed her in the light of day as well as the dark of night? Where else but the bedchamber could he mean? Surely, not outside? And in what manner could he mean than lying together as men and women did? She cursed her ignorance in those matters. Her head shook even as she gave her consent. "Aye."

"So, what do you offer that I do not have, Annora?" His

voice surrounded her and heated her from within. "If, *when*, I win, you will belong to me in all ways that matter. To do with or to dispose of how I please." He let those words settle in for a moment. "So, what of value do you offer me personally?"

"I will aid you in defeating le Govic however I can."

"Since you cannot pick up a lance and ride at my side, what are you proposing?" He released her then and stepped back. Her body noticed the loss of his warmth immediately. "Do you think that a traitor is also a cheater?"

"Nay!" She reached out and touched his sleeve to stop his retreat. "I but meant that I would share with you anything I learn about my father and le Govic's plans. I suspect they, even if not traitors, have no compunction about cheating."

"I could already have someone working close to le Govic, informing me about such things."

"Do you plan to challenge every offer I make?" She let out her exasperation in a breath.

"Do you plan to offer something I do not have at my disposal in exchange for agreeing to your terms?" he asked her, repeating her words and tone. "I think we both realize that once the deed is done, when I win and you are mine by the king's decree and consent, I do not have to make any concessions to you at all."

She gasped at his boldness and yet, she could not deny the truth of his words. She would be at his mercy. She met his eyes then and realized that she did not doubt he had mercy within his soul, while she knew to a certainty that le Govic had none.

"What do you offer me, Lady Annora?"

The silence grew between them. The sounds of the camp settling down for the night pierced into their own small peace. Then, even though she was sure he already knew what she would offer, she spoke the words.

"In addition to any knowledge or news I hear?"

He nodded.

"Me. I offer myself to you. Whenever you wish. Now, if you'd like."

Annora could not look directly at him. Her palms sweated, and a nervous trickle slid down her spine. Rubbing her hands against her gown, her thighs trembled in response. Her body felt strange—awake and alarmed at the same time. Anticipation filled her as she waited for his answer. For his...attentions. From the way he'd behaved since their first meeting, she had little doubt that he would have his way with her within moments of accepting her offer.

"Fine, my lady. I accept your offer," he said, his voice even deeper than its usual tone. "Now..."

Annora held her breath as she waited for his command. Would he take her on the pallet? Would it be now? Or as le Govic had tried from behind? The strangest, most unbelievable thing was that she did not fear Thomas doing that, doing this, with him. Indeed, and shamefully, she admitted to herself, she wanted to know the feel of him. The feel of his flesh in her palm. The feel of his hand on her body, holding her breast without the layers of gown and chemise between them.

"Get on the pallet."

Annora turned and walked to the corner where the pallet was. For a temporary bed in a temporary tent, it looked more than comfortable with its piles of pillows and furs and blankets. 'Twas a king's tent, so such amenities were to be expected. Once she reached the bedding, she stopped and turned to face Thomas, awaiting his next command. 'Twas something she must accustom herself to if he was to be her master after he won.

"Get on the pallet, Annora," he repeated in a soft voice.

Should she disrobe first? Did he wish her to remain clothed for this encounter? He nodded his head towards the pallet, so she knelt on it and then sat.

"Your side is against the wall of the tent," he explained as he approached.

She slid over, pushing the blankets out of her way.

"Lie down."

No matter how calmly he spoke, it did nothing to ease her worries now. Would he take her virtue as the price of sealing their bargain? Could she even believe he would honor their agreement once he won? Should she trust the word of a traitor? She would learn soon enough. She eased back, sliding one of the pillows behind her head as she did.

"Now, go to sleep," he said as he tossed her cloak to her.

"I do not understand," she said. Sitting up, she shook her head. "Have you changed your decision about our arrangement, then?"

"Nay, lady, I have not."

"Then? Will you not take what I offer you?"

The man lifted his head and stared at the top of the tent, his lips moving, but few sounds escaped. She heard the whispered words calling on the Almighty. He was praying?

She waited on the pallet in respectful silence as he finished, but the words he uttered when he opened his eyes to look at her did not sound like a prayer at all. They sounded like a curse instead. Foul words that no lady, and most men, would not say. But he did. She winced at the awful sound of them.

And he gazed directly at her as he did.

"Annora, lie down and get some rest," he said. "The morn will come soon enough, and you must be ready to sneak back into the keep if we hope to hide this little escapade and our arrangement from your father's view."

"Truly?"

He'd confounded her once more. She did not doubt that he desired her, for she had seen his flesh rise beneath his breeches when she'd made the offer to him. It pressed against the fabric with every word he'd spoken about *having* her. Even now as she glanced there once again, it remained—

"Annora! Stop staring at my prick!"

First, she covered her eyes, and then she covered her mouth. Never in her life had she behaved in such an indecent manner. And yet, so far in one day at this tournament, she had recklessly kissed a man and let him fondle her, spied on an intimate encounter and seen his...prick, and offered herself and her virtue to a man who had been trying to take it every time they'd met. She stared now at that very same erect flesh right there in front of her.

When she tried to look away and not stare again at the growing size of it, he did the most unexpected thing—he laughed. Oh, but she loved the sound of his laughter. Its deep tones permeated her entire body and warmed her soul. He laughed fully and without reserve, like a man who'd faced death and come out with a new appreciation of life. And hadn't he done just that? Annora could not help but drop her hands from their futile attempt to shield her gaze and laugh with him.

Ten

Good God, she was amazing to watch.

When she should have been quaking in terror at the thought of giving up the only thing she could rightfully claim as her own to a man like him, she sat—on his bed—laughing with full abandon. Then, he caught her staring and they both saw the result of that inquisitive gaze. She continued to look at him, and he felt his cock standing more with each moment she did.

Yet watching her laugh now for the first time in his presence, he realized, Thomas just wanted to drink in the sight and sound of it. Which could only lead to trouble for both of them. He'd agreed to her bargain, but he could not reconcile taking her virtue as part of that. The tiny remnant of his honorable self left intact, after he'd lost most of himself in the process of being a traitor and the punishing deprivation that he'd faced, could simply not allow him to take it..

She dragged her the back of her hand across her eyes then, her laughter bringing tears to her eyes as his laughter had and smiled. "I will seek my rest now."

Sliding back down onto the pillows and arranging her cloak to cover her, Annora smiled once more and he regretted every bit of control he had. After she tugged more furs and blankets over her, Thomas watched her as she settled, turning on her side to face the side of the tent next to the pallet. He'd thought her finally asleep when she spoke.

"Where will you sleep?" Annora leaned up on her elbows and looked at him over the pile of bedcovers.

"I doubt I will."

"Do you not need your rest for the battles to come?"

"I am touched by your concern, my lady." He nodded and turned away, seeking out the chair that was the farthest from the pallet. "When my body requires it, I have been known to find sleep anywhere. Even a chair." Thomas sat down and put his feet up on the nearby stool. Then, he crossed his arms over his chest, leaned his head back and closed his eyes.

"Very well," she said.

He did not open his eyes to see if she lay back down, for the noise she made as she did was clear. Soon, only the sound of her soft, even breathing filled the tent. Listening to her, he thought on her offer and her seeming indignation when he did not take her as she'd thought he would.

The rhythmic rise and fall of her breaths as they echoed around him calmed him. So much needed yet to be done. Final practices with his horse and final preparations to make. Two other challenges before he faced le Govic on behalf of his king. As he had in the past, Thomas concentrated on only the next thing he must accomplish. He never allowed himself to think too far ahead once his overall goal was established. Each step deserved his complete attention. Overthinking was his enemy.

The sounds of the camp rousing to life for another day filled with the fighting and drinking and wenching of those here for the tournament stirred him. When he'd fallen asleep, he knew not. Wiping his hands over his eyes,

Thomas stretched and rose.

"Come, Annora. We must get you back inside before you can be seen." Glancing over, he found that the pallet was empty. The tent was empty, save for him.

Annora was gone.

Luck or the Almighty was finally on her side.

Annora managed to make it out of the tent, away from Thomas, away from any servants and back to the gate of the town before dawn's light fully illuminated the sky and the camp. Scurrying with her hood up and her head down, she entered the keep and found her way to the small chamber assigned to her. Margaret slept on her pallet in the corner, though from her appearance, it would seem she did not rest well. The girl was dressed, with even her shoes in place, and lay on her crumpled cloak. As Annora closed the door behind her, the maid woke.

"My lady! I searched for you everywhere," Margaret said. "I thought mayhap you attended to your personal needs, but the garderobes were empty, as were the corridors."

"Did you send for my father or alert anyone else?" Annora untied her cloak and let it drop on the bed. "Does anyone else know I left this chamber?" When the maid did not answer, Annora turned to her. "'Tis important, Margaret. Did you speak to anyone else about this?"

But Margaret was staring at Annora's neck instead of speaking. The bruises must look as bad as they felt this morning. She sighed.

"My lady! Who did that to you?" Margaret whispered. "Did your father...beat you so?"

Annora decided to let that lie stand for now. Before she could say more, a loud knock interrupted them. Margaret went to open it, and Annora took advantage of that to readjust the edge of her gown and to tug her braid over her shoulder to cover the handprint.

"My lady." Annora looked up to find her father's servant there. "Your father sent me to bring you to his tent."

"I have only just risen, as the sun has," she said. Smiling at the man, she tried to gain more time. "I must wash and dress properly before I can leave this chamber or keep."

"My lady, he sent us," the man pointed to three others she'd not seen at first glance, "to bring your trunks and belongings over to the camp. He wishes you at his side and to stay there for the rest of the tournament."

"But the baron invited me to stay here," she explained. "Surely, my father would not turn down the baron's hospitality?"

"My lady, I am sent to bring you and your belongings to his tent. We will wait out here until you are ready." The man stepped back into the corridor, and Margaret would have closed the door but for his raised hand against it. "My lady?"

"What is it now? We will prepare as quickly as possible." The man did not reply but tilted his head in an effort to have her approach. Annora did, understanding he had something else, something more private to say.

"Your father is in a foul mood and filled with impatience." He paused and lowered his voice once more. "I would not dawdle or delay in readying yourself and your maid to answer his call."

Annora nodded and closed the door. What had caused her father's temper to flare? Did he know she'd been in the camp overnight? That she had encountered his champion? Or worse, that Thomas had intervened? Had le Govic truly had his permission to avail himself of her favors, so now her father was angry that she'd not given in to him?

It took only a short while to prepare herself. The guard's words and manner alarmed her, and she rushed Margaret to pack. Soon, she followed her father's men down through the keep, the town and out the gate that led to the campground.

The fields were more crowded now, as hundreds had arrived for the tournament. The excitement had grown as it became known that several of the knights who would fight were undefeated in battle. That seemed to bring out even additional challenges and more people to watch to see if those knights would fall this time.

Far off into the distance away from the town's walls, tents of all colors and sizes covered the fields like wildflowers in the spring. The traffic on the road, both to and from the town, moved slowly now as many made their way to the stands to watch the jousts. Well-dressed and well-accompanied ladies with their entourages of admirers and servants and kin, followed by town folk and always the merchants who sought to make a living, filled the paths off the road to the lines and lines of tents. Though they'd hurried along the way, her father's greeting was less than cordial when they did arrive.

"Why did you not heed my call, Annora?" he asked. His expression was a mix of sternness and anger, but the calm of his voice frightened her more. She was lowering into a curtsy when Sir Laurence moved in the shadows, distracting her. "Her willfulness has never pleased me, le Govic. 'Tis something you will have to attend to when she is in your care if it bothers you as much as it does me."

Annora shivered as she lowered herself then. Her father spoke as though it was accomplished already and did not depend on any joust yet to be called.

"Father, I pray you, forgive me for my tardiness," she said, bowing her head. "The crowds slowed us as we left the town."

Annora closed her eyes and held her breath, waiting for the blow to land, for her father's methods were known to her. When it came not, she inhaled before looking up. He reached over and moved her braid.

"I do not want you marked so," he said. "Too many prying eyes. Too many who would ask questions here." Suddenly the bruises on her neck ached as her father stared at them. "Le Govic, was that not my order to you?"

"Aye, my lord, it was." The knight came closer and stood at her father's side. The violent gleam in his eyes frightened her. "But she did not obey me."

"You will have plenty of time to correct her after the tournament. For now, keep your distance."

"Aye, my lord." Le Govic nodded and then gave her a look that promised when the time came, he would do exactly what he wanted to her.

If that time came, she prayed. Annora shuddered again before looking back at her father.

"What did you do after Brisbois interfered?" Stunned by the admission included in her father's words, Annora could not speak. "What did you do, Annora?"

"I ran back to the keep," she lied. "I got back inside the walls just after the curfew was called."

"Well, you will remain here with me for the rest of the tournament. I am having another tent set for your use. Set her trunks there for now," he ordered his guard. "Get her dressed more appropriately for the coming jousts," he said, directing that order to her maid. "Her champion has been challenged this day, and she must cheer him on in the stands."

Her father walked away to speak to the man who would defend his honor, and her fear was such that she almost missed a small interaction between the two men. When her father began speaking in low tones to le Govic, the knight turned and faced her father with his other side. 'Twas not to block her from seeing their conversation, for it put them in a position where she could see their expressions clearly. She did not know why it struck her as strange, but it did.

"Bring her when she is prepared," her father said to the guard as he and le Govic left.

"You there," Margaret said as soon as Annora's father was gone. "You bring some food so that the lady can break her fast." The guard at whom she aimed her orders looked as though he would refuse until Annora nodded. "And you, bring those trunks away from the side of the tent where rain could ruin them."

Annora waited while Margaret issued a few more commands about her lady's safety and comfort and established herself in the hierarchy of servants before allowing Margaret to dress her once more, in one of her finest chemises and kirtles. This time, Margaret arranged her hair and wisely used a wimple to cover her neck. After her maid placed a veil over that and used a circlet to hold it all in place, Annora stood to leave. Margaret held out a wispy bit of fabric to her.

"Put this in your sleeve, my lady," she said.

Another veil.

"I do not wish to *favor* le Govic," she admitted softly.

"What you wish to do and what you will do are two different matters, my lady."

Annora stared at the bit of material that would say so much and willed herself to take it. She must play her part, even while she hoped Thomas would play his. Accepting it and easing it up under the edge of her sleeve, Annora nodded.

"When did you become so wise, Margaret?"

Annora drew in a last deep breath before nodding to Margaret to lift the flap of the tent for her. At this point, she had taken the only step she could to control her fate, and now she must wait to see it through. If, *if* things went as badly as they could, she would belong to Le Govic at the end of this tournament, so raising his ire was not the smart thing to do. With all that in mind, she forced a smile on her face and stepped outside.

The layers of fabric that made up her father's tent had blocked much of the sounds and sun, and Annora stood in shock at the loudness and brightness that surrounded her now. A nod at the waiting guard had him begin their walk to the place in the stands where her father awaited her. Though Margaret followed close behind, Annora felt isolated and alone as they moved through the teeming mass of people who gathered near to and in the area leading to the lists.

Even though terror filled her at the thought of what could happen, she could not fight the rising excitement of seeing so many people and hearing so many familiar and unfamiliar voices and accents. The highest and lowest of several lands were here now, and she tried to concentrate on the guard ahead of her as they moved on. Just as in the market yesterday, it was hard not to be overwhelmed by the scents and colors, and the sounds of horns and clashing swords and cheering.

It took some time for them to make their way from the area where most of the tents were located over to the lists where the jousts and fighting took place. Lord Yves had built three long fields of honor that were next to more practice fields and the stabling area. In the other direction was an area she'd been warned about—a large and rather rough makeshift tavern stood nearer the river, along with the place where women sold their wares and themselves. Her father and le Govic had been coming from that direction when he'd intercepted her. A shiver of revulsion shook her at just the fleeting memory of that.

She could see that her guard escorted her towards the large viewing stand where nobles and honored guests could watch the fighting from a platform above where most stood. Once more, ladies in all colors and styles gathered, cooing over the knights who rode and fought before them, as those who stood below shouted out both encouragement and curses. The jousts that were part of the tournament had begun the day before, and already there was talk of who would win the final prize heard her father calling out to her from ahead, and she peeked around the guard to see him. He was speaking to Lord Yves but stopped as she approached.

So much intrigue swirled around them, and Annora prayed that she would not suffer more for the choices these powerful men made. Whispers she'd overheard before leaving home about the true puppeteer behind this whole endeavor made her nervous. With the king yet across the sea, his ambitious brother was let loose on England, forming strange and secret alliances that even a woman as sheltered as she'd been could tell were portends of trouble. Annora reached the baron's place and curtsied to him and her father.

"Here she is now, Baron de la Rose. Annora, since our champion is fighting this morn, Lord Yves has reserved a place for you at his side."

"I am honored, my lord," she said as she stepped over to the open seat there and sat. Her father returned to his place on Lord Yves's other side, and their whispers continued unabated until le Govic's name was called out by the herald.

"He has a full morning of challenges, I've been told," the baron said to her father, now speaking openly.

"Le Govic is not cowardly like some others who will fight here," her father boasted as a shudder trembled through her. Keeping a smile in place was growing harder by the moment. "He will fight and defeat anyone who comes before him."

Annora could not hear Lord Yves's reply, but she met his frank stare at her as her father boasted. She broadened her smile and nodded in what she hoped was an appropriate manner until he turned his wise gaze away.

"Here, he comes now!" her father said as he leapt to his feet and clapped as the dangerous man and his opponent approached the stand.

Though given a full introduction, Annora was so distracted by worry that all she could remember was that le Govic's opponent was a knight from England named Robert of…someplace. As the rules were pronounced once more to all, le Govic raked her with his hot and lustful gaze—from the top of her head down to her toes. She could almost feel his grasping fingers digging into her skin and the tight hold on her neck as he did.

"Lady Annora?" Lord Yves's deep voice broke into her thoughts. "Your champion would like a token from you."

Eleven

Le Govic moved closer to the railing and held out his lance in her direction. His mount snorted and tried to rear up, as obnoxious in his behavior as his rider. Le Govic's smile now was more a leer than anything else. Knowing she must play her part while she prayed for the outcome she needed, Annora reached into her sleeve and pulled out the small wisp of veil that Margaret, God bless the woman, had urged her to take.

"Sir Laurence," she said, nodding at him as her stomach threatened to rebel. "I wish you a successful battle." *And may your opponents drive you to the ground and batter you to pieces.* With her false smile firmly in place, she reached over and tied the token on his offered lance.

"I will bring you—us—great honor, my lady," he called out. She tried to control her reaction to his words, especially his use of the word *honor*, but thought the wince might have been seen. Her father's rough pinch to the back of her arm told her so. Annora straightened up and nodded.

Though the cheering from the crowd watching covered most of what he said, Annora's father whispered into her ear. In every word, she heard the sound of her father's desperation, for clearly, he was involved in something that was about more than this affair. Even more dangerous than tying her future to that of Le Govic.

Something dark swirled around them here at this momentous gathering. Something that seemed to involve the very balance of power among kingdoms and nobles. A whispered word here. A suspicious glance there. Small conclaves where words were guarded. Oh, something was going on here at Lord Yves's tournament, and Annora knew her father was in it deeply.

Soon, the thunderous pounding of the horses' hooves echoed in her own heart, and she turned her attention to the two knights there on the field. Le Govic was bigger than his opponent, but the other knight did not hesitate to charge him. She prepared for the crash of the lances into armor as they drew closer, and even knowing it would happen did not diminish the shock of it.

Gasps, shouts and cries filled the air as those watching jumped to their feet as they waited to see if either man would fall. The crowd's keen disappointment echoed across the lists as both men kept their seats, lances unbroken, and looked none worse for it. It took little time for the le Govic and Sir Robert to return to their starting places and begin their charge once more. Annora held her breath and prayed.

Le Govic injured so that he could compete no more. She would have wished for a more permanent end, but she dared not tempt the Almighty with such a plea. So, le Govic knocked senseless on the ground, with possibly a broken arm, was what she asked for instead. Truly, any injury that would prevent him from fighting with Thomas or hinder his chances of winning against the man she wanted to win.

This next round resulted in the loud breaking of Sir Robert's lance, giving points and applause to the man. When le Govic raised the shield of his helm, his displeasure was clear. He'd expected to deliver a quick defeat to his English opponent, and his angry expression turned even darker as the victorious knight waved to those cheering for him.

Though of short acquaintance, Annora had seen what le Govic did when his aims were thwarted. Her hand touched the bruises on her neck before she knew it. A shudder trembled through her, and she tried to hide it by adjusting her wimple.

The call for the knights to begin came, and those watching cheered anew. Once more, Annora stared ahead and prepared herself for the deafening sounds—hooves, weapons, lances and the shouting of spectators. Splintering wood against metal forced her gaze to the two knights, and she nearly shouted her joy when she noticed that le Govic's opponent had won points in the encounter. Though not unseated, le Govic looked shaken.

One could not take a lance to the chest without being worse for it, even if wearing armor. No dents were obvious, but any number of injuries and faults could be hidden from view by their surcoats. As she knew, no warrior wished to display their weaknesses while still in battle. And this was nothing less than a battle.

It took longer for le Govic to regain his balance, and for a moment—one not long enough for her—it looked as though he might fall. But he pulled himself up straight on the saddle and nodded that he was ready.

One more hit like this one could unseat him. One good blow could take him down. Annora uncharitably prayed for those things as the two men took their places at opposite ends of the lists and paused, awaiting the signal to begin.

The rules of this tournament were not rules of battle, for no one was attempting to kill their opponents. Well, in truth, some were, but the majority here were simply trying to prove their superiority over others and win prizes, wealth, lands, brides and ransom. One could not enjoy the fruits of their labor if they were dead. So, after three broken lances, if there were no clear winner, they would continue on the ground.

Annora begged silently once more that it would be ended, that *he* would be ended, with this next and, hopefully, last pass. As both horses began to stamp and paw the ground in anticipation, Annora could not breathe. Everything, her whole future could change with this one ride. She gazed at le Govic's opponent and hoped he would be able to bring her torment to an end. The signal was given and...the horses gathered their powerful haunches and burst forward down the lane.

She alternately could not watch and yet had to, opening and closing her eyes in a series of peeks, until the warriors were in the final yards. Then, paralyzed with fear, she watched the last few seconds and saw her hopes come to an end.

Le Govic managed to get a direct hit on his opponent, one that was so strong it pushed Sir Robert off his horse, landed him on the ground and knocked him senseless. When the dust settled, there was a moment of complete silence, and then a wave of cheering and shouting began to move through the crowds. It seemed to pause, but when the knight moved his arm—indicating that he lived—the wave rose and crashed over them all.

Le Govic rode along the stands smiling at the adoration pouring forth for him now, passing her several times with nary a glance. The only good thing from this was that he might seek out the company of others to celebrate this triumph and keep from her. With the other knight yet before them on the ground, le Govic jumped from his horse and stood before Lord Yves and waited for the herald to announce his victory.

Annora glanced away for a moment, her gaze moving across the three fields of honor to the far fence where a number of other knights had gathered to watch. The tallest of them drew her eye and she could swear he was looking at her, too. Then, he shook his head and turned, stalking off into the crowd and out of her sight.

For some reason, that quick, determined exit from the field disheartened her more than le Govic's win here. The knight did not look back, not at the fields nor in her direction, and soon he disappeared into the line of tents and the milling crowds.

Despair trickled into her fearful heart now. Le Govic was impressive in his fight. Annora settled back in the chair and continued watching as he took on three more challengers that day. Any attempt on her part to leave, even for sustenance or comfort, was met with refusal on her father's part. Was he punishing her for refusing the man's attempts to take her? Or just showing his domination over her before the powerful baron?

Hours later, as le Govic, winded and exhausted, accepted the congratulations of Lord Yves and the adoration of many willing women around her, she understood her father's message.

There was no way out of this for her.

She'd nearly given up all hope as he beat Sir Robert, then Sir George and then battled Sir Dougal. But something tickled her thoughts as she watched him recover and reposition and ready himself for the next ride. Something was wrong here, yet she could not make sense of what bothered her about the way he fought. Nay, she could not narrow down what made her suspicious, but she knew there was something. Somehow it was connected to his action in their tent earlier.

Something was not right.

Pray God, she would sort it out before Thomas faced

him on the field for their challenge on behalf of the Scottish king

Pray God.

At Lord Yves's third request, her father relented and sent her off to eat and "refresh herself" in their tent, with a demand for her swift return. Although the nobleman had invited her to supper in the hall, her father managed to refuse without insulting their host. Somehow, the enigmatic lord did get him to agree she could break her fast in the hall in the morning. The reason for that, she knew not, but then having accomplished something he apparently wanted, the baron turned his attention to a few of the other honored guests and allowed his probing gaze to move elsewhere.

Did Lord Yves know her true feelings in the matter? Was he part of her father's questionable plan here at the tourney? Sadly, she had no true idea of what enterprise her father was involved in with others. Should she worry? She could do nothing to influence her father in this, nor could she ask him to explain his part, or that of Prince John's or any of the others who seemed drawn into this matter.

Lives, ones more important than hers, were at stake when kings clashed or plotted.

Once freed from her father's tight grasp, she found Margaret and went over to the place where vendors sold their food and filled her belly. All the while, she kept watching to see if Thomas would appear. Though he'd left the field after le Govic's first victory, she did not believe he'd simply walked away. There was too much at stake for him to give up the chance of watching his opponent face others at varying levels of skill and experience. Even if they had fought before...

The crumbs of the meat pie caught in her throat then, and

she coughed to clear them. After Margaret slammed her hand on Annora's back several times, and after a mouthful of ale, the blockage was gone, and Annora could think once more.

These two men had met in battle or on the field before. From the bits of conversation and whispered words she'd overheard, even when Thomas first came to Prudhoe Castle, she knew they had known each other and fought before. And yet, it had never entered her mind to ask him about it.

Well, truthfully, once in his tent, there were other matters to discuss. Other arrangements to make. Her body reacted to the memories of their encounter, and heat spread through her. Annora closed her eyes and tried to banish those errant desires. When she opened them, 'twas as though her thoughts had conjured him up before her.

"My lady," he said in a soft tone as he claimed a place at her side on the bench on which she sat. To Annora's amazement, Margaret nodded at him and left without a word or glance at her.

"Sir."

He gazed at her with a challenge in his dark brown eyes.

She met it. "How is it that you control *my* maid?" Much to her annoyance, jealousy entered her tone. She cleared her throat. "Why would Margaret leave without my permission?"

There. That sounded less suspicious, but only the tone had changed, not the wave of jealousy that pierced her at the idea that Thomas and her own maid were somehow connected. And remembering the words and praises of the women she'd overheard speaking about him, why did her mind go to *that* reason as the only possibility? She let out a sigh then, not wishing to believe herself jealous of her maid while feeling the burn of it coursing through her veins.

"Fear not, my lady. I but asked her for some time alone with you," he said.

Before she could speak, he slid his hand over hers on the rough wooden table and moved them both to the space, the very small space, between them on the bench. The gasp that escaped her as he entwined their fingers and rested their hands on her leg could not be helped. Glancing around, she hoped no one would notice his action or her reaction.

"I assure you that you hold her loyalty."

Annora tried to disengage her hand, but he only tightened his grasp. And her attempt simply made his hand slide along her thigh as he held on. A sudden tightness gathered within her at the intimate touch.

"Why have you sent her away then? If we have nothing to fear from her?"

"I would speak to you alone."

He lifted their hands to his mouth then, and he kissed hers before she could stop him. It took a few moments before she realized he'd released hers, and it yet remained near his mouth as though wanting more. And she could not want more!

Or so she would tell herself.

But the way her body ached at his nearness and the way her skin itched to be touched made her a liar then. If he won, when he won, he would touch her. Every part of her body would be his to caress and kisses and... At any time. In any place.

"Are you well, Lady Annora? You look a bit overheated." The playful tone in his question made it clear that he knew the effect he had on her now. "The sun's light is strong today. Mayhap you would like to walk in the shade a bit? Over there?" He nodded towards the river where the tall trees along its edge moved in the breezes. He'd stood and began helping her up before she thought to object. Then she did.

"I do not think that is an appropriate place to walk," she

said. Just past the food carts and vendors lay the makeshift tavern and past that lay the place where certain women plied their trade.

"We will go no farther than the water's edge there."

He held out his arm, and she placed her hand on it, and they walked. She would have preferred to simply remove the wimple from her head for it held all the heat in, but then she would chance exposing the bruises on her neck. And then the questions would follow, not from her father for he knew what had happened, but from others. So, she hoped the cooler breezes would help her.

Annora watched Thomas from the corner of her eyes as they made their way along the edge of the tables set up there. Though many glances were thrown in his direction, by men and women alike, he neither called out nor acknowledged any of them.

Thomas seemed to know his path, and soon they stood by the edge of the river and in the shade of the tall trees. He led her to a low branch that seemed to reach out towards the flowing waters nearby and waited while she sat. After making certain they were alone, Annora pulled the circlet and veil from her head and tugged the wimple free from the edge of her gown, exposing her neck and braided hair. The cool air soothed her at once, and she could not help the sigh she let out at the feel of it moving over her heated skin.

"Now imagine the pleasure of such breezes moving over our skin, slick from making love by a river such as this," he said in a voice no more than a whisper. "I would pleasure you and take you over and over and then allow the breezes to cool the heat of your skin when we finished."

Annora felt the immediate results of his words, his promise, his invitation, deep within her body as the place at her core began to throb. Her breasts ached and swelled, and she wanted him to cup them as he had in the dark alcove in the castle.

"I would strip you naked, Annora. I would spread your hair around you and watch as it gleamed in the sunlight." He had not moved, but her body flushed with the pleasure of his touch. "I think I will enjoy seeing you so."

The way her mouth gaped open then could not be enticing, yet it did not stop him from continuing his provocative words.

"Can you swim?" he asked.

So caught up in his arousing description, she did not realize he was waiting for her to answer. A nod would have to suffice.

"Ah, good." His wide mouth curved into that hungry predator's smile she'd seen at their first meeting. "I want to take you in the water. Naked. In a calm place where the current is not strong. I will lift you up and wrap your legs around my waist and enter you like that."

Now, the place between her legs clenched at the thought of his possession. "You should not speak so," she said, her voice quivering with these new feelings of longing and craving.

"I must remember that you are indeed a lady and a maiden one and not accustomed to talking about such things."

His gaze met hers, and she could read frank desire in it. No malice. No harm. Just a demand that her body understood. His smile changed then into something warmer and less dangerous, and yet her instincts did not allow her to be at ease.

"But, Annora, when you are mine, you will allow it. We will speak of matters such as these, and you will acquiesce to my commands. You gave your word in agreeing to our arrangement."

How could his simple words, without closeness or touch, affect her so? An urge to run to him across the small distance between them grew as her body heated, and the hunger for those scandalous deeds nearly overwhelmed her. Here. Now.

Nay!

She could blame her lack of control on her inexperience in matters such as pleasure and passion. Glancing at Thomas, she realized he did not appear undisciplined. He looked sure of himself as one did when certain of their actions and their plans. Not inflamed to recklessness as she felt at this moment. Annora must learn from him, or she would put the power to destroy her in his hands willingly. And this whole bargain with him was to avoid that. To keep some semblance of control over her choices, and her life, within her own grasp.

So, Annora shook herself and took a deep breath meant to ease the tension inside her. When she felt as confident as he appeared, and in spite of the arousal yet coursing through her body, she met his gaze. And asked the very question that had been plaguing her just before he appeared at her side.

"So, tell me, Thomas, how did le Govic beat you the last time you fought him?"

Twelve

He would deny it to the instant of his death, but Thomas was certain he squawked like a chicken when she blurted out her question. One moment, she was glorious in her arousal and the next, she targeted her words to his weakness with the expertise of a king's bowman. He laughed again as it made her frown.

"You should laugh more often, sir."

Now it was his brow that raised. "Me? Laugh more? Why, my lady?"

"You look a..." She paused and shook her head as though she'd changed her intention and then shrugged. "So, tell me about you and le Govic."

"Let us get to the heart of the matter then, my lady?" Thomas walked to her and sat on the sturdy branch. As that the glow of the desire between them had burnt away, he could chance being nearer to her. "What is it you wish to know?"

"I mean no disrespect," she said, shifting a bit, so she almost faced him. "I cannot offer suggestions or help if I do not know anything about you and him. How does your method of fighting differ from his? Are the lance and horse your strength, or do you prefer the sword on the ground?

How did he manage to defeat you last time?"

How many times could she surprise him? It seemed that she did in their every encounter, and twice so far in this one. Those words coming from another would be an insult at best and an invitation to death at worst. Yet, when she spoke them—and questioned his abilities, his experience and possibly his honor—he heard the honest curiosity in her voice. More, they were intelligent questions likely to force him to examine all three things..

"This morn was the first time I have watched him fight since we did."

"When was that? From my father's comments and such, it seems like a long time ago?"

"'Twas fifteen years ago." Yet, it was never far from his thoughts these days.

"Had he challenged you or was this less formal?" she asked.

"We were sparring. Practicing, when it changed."

Annora let out a loud sigh and shook her head at his reply. "If I have to ask you for each detail of it like this, the tournament will be over, and the matter decided," she said with a sharpness in her tone that bespoke of her impatience with prideful men. Or mayhap stupid ones. "Will you just tell me how it happened? Had you met in battle before that?"

Thomas met her perceptive gaze and then stared out at the river as its water rushed by them. If only it were that easy to explain. If he could just tell her the whole of it and let her judge. If he could... Looking at her now, for the first time since it happened and in spite of years of being questioned over it and reminded of it and hating it, Thomas wanted to tell her all of it.

She made him want to expose his secrets and his weaknesses and his longings to her. She made him want her in ways that challenged everything within himself. But, life and the near loss of his had taught him a hard lesson in trusting secrets to others. He turned back to her.

"Suffice to say that we were young and foolish men practicing, insults were offered, fighting ensued. At the end of things, I ended up disgraced in the dirt with a broken jaw."

He would have been fine in keeping that resolution of distance between them if she'd not reached up and caressed his jaw, as though searching for the old injury. Mayhap if he'd just taken her last night in his tent when she was so very ready to give him her maidenhead, he could have satisfied this growing need for her. Too late now for such questions. The touch of her soft hand and the damned concern in her blue-green eyes broke him and his control.

Too late.

Thomas reached over and pulled her to him. There was a moment when he could have released her, but when she stared at his mouth and leaned in towards him, he gathered her closer and kissed the breath out of her. When she inhaled another, he kissed that one from her and over and over until they were both breathless and panting.

His cock, hard and needy, urged him to find a place of privacy. His mouth craved her taste. His skin ached to lie naked upon hers and feel the luscious curves she hid beneath her kirtle and gown. His hands slid down from her shoulders to caress her back and hold her.

Then, sadly for the rest of his body's parts and places, his wits returned and reminded him of their location and the dangers of being discovered like this together. Thomas eased his way back a few inches that seemed like miles. Her lips were red and swollen from his kisses, and he felt insanely good about that. He glanced away for a moment and then nodded at her.

"I have not seen le Govic fight again until this day. He

was impressive." The little intake of breath spoke of her dismay, and he continued, "but I do not think he has seen me fight since, either. He is arrogant, stubborn and prideful, and it will be his downfall."

When Thomas met her gaze, he recognized confusion and passion awakening and fear there. His words were not the most comforting or filled with the confidence she wanted to hear. But then, she did not understand him or how he approached a challenge or faced a threat. He'd thought her pragmatic in coming to him with her own offer to seek an arrangement in which her future was protected.

Well, he did not hold to inflated confidence, whether in his training for battle or in accepting this situation. His first reaction after managing to stand before the king and hear his demands was to try to convince William of the folly of it. But a king being a king and completely convinced that his subjects, especially ones facing imminent death, should do his bidding, would brook no refusal from him.

Now, he must deal with a different sort of opponent here. One who offered her aid to him, even while they battled. So, if she'd offered, he would have to accept, would he not?

"Tell me what you saw when he fought."

"Truly?" she asked. Her eyes brightened, and some of the fear left them.

At his nod, she settled more comfortably at his side and gave her assessment freely. He tried to pay heed to her words, but her mannerisms as she spoke captured his attention. The way her smile gave away her joy at being given leave to advise him. The manner in which her eyes sparkled as she offered her counsel. The soft touch of her hand on his sleeve as she described a move that le Govic had made during the second challenge.

How had she made him want her so much in such a short time? And, although he wanted her in his bed—with complete freedom and control over her body—Thomas could sense a growing need of a different kind. One that made him want her intelligence and her keen sense of observation and her skills at piecing patterns together and pulling them apart. She ran her father's demesne and was experienced in all manner and number of things.

She would make a nobleman the perfect...

Thomas shook himself out of that path of thinking and stood abruptly, startling himself and the lady. Annora stared up at him.

"Are you well, Thomas? You look..." After a pause, she nodded. Annora stood then and narrowed her gaze as she studied his face. "Ill?" Her words repeated his own to her with that slight change, and he smiled as he held out his hand to her.

"I am well, and I am late to meet someone," he said, giving the weakest excuse he'd ever given. "May I escort you back to Margaret so you may return together to wherever it is that your father expects to find you?"

Annora smoothed her hair, replaced her wimple and circlet and then took his arm and allowed his escort back towards the carts and vendors. He nodded to the maid, who stood waiting for her lady. Before they reached her, Annora pulled them to a halt.

"I wanted to wish you luck in your challenges on the morrow," she said. "I am certain you will win both." She let out a sigh then. "I would offer you a token if I could." She touched her sleeve as though she thought something there.

"Nay. 'Twould be too dangerous to allow our liaison known."

"A liaison, was it?" she asked, a hint of humor underlying her words. He covered her hand where it rested on his arm and nodded.

"When a woman slips into a man's tent in the dark of

night and remains there until dawn, in his bed—" He raised his brow and winked at her. "'Tis a liaison, my lady."

The blush that filled her cheeks then made him want to undress her to see if that becoming pink colored the skin on her breasts. Oh, she would be splendid to take to bed and discover what would draw out that enhancing color and sighs and moans.

She must have sensed the rising arousal between them, for she ran off then, leaving him to watch her go. He slid his hand inside his tunic and touched the veil he'd hidden there. He knew if he drew it to his nose, he would smell the scent of her. He had done it already...many times.

When she'd disappeared through the crowds, Thomas turned in the direction of his tent. He needed to prepare for his challenges in the morn. The two knights who'd challenged him were fair in their skills and their reputations. Neither would be less than a good fight, but neither would give him much of a problem. The two would serve as good practice and preparing his skills on the morrow to be ready to face le Govic the following day.

He reached his tent, feeling confident about the next day. And mayhap the next two.

The thunder rumbling overhead woke him before his servant could. As he lay there listening, the winds grew louder and pounded against the sides of the tent, threatening to tear them apart. His stomach churned as he heard the rains that struck the ground in waves, driven by those damned winds and made worse by the rolling thunder that shook the ground. The only thing missing was the...

A bright, blinding flash of lightning lit outside and inside the tent then.

Thomas sat up and rubbed his head roughly. Leaning

his elbows on his knees, now drawn up to his chest, he could not believe it. Last evening when he'd retired, there were few clouds in the darkening skies to portend this kind of storm.

He had few, if any, choices in this. The challenges on the lists would go on, fair weather or foul. If the one challenged withdrew, they lost whatever was at stake. If the challenger did it, there was no loss of reputation or goods or gold. He let out a vicious curse, at the weather, at the Almighty, at the king and even at his own stupidity for believing this would all work out to his advantage. Neither of the men who challenged him would withdraw and miss this chance to fight him. He knew them both well enough to know that.

Before he got off the pallet to dress, Martel entered the tent and, even in the midst of his frustration at the conditions, it gave Thomas pleasure to see the man dripping wet.

"The challenges will go on in spite of the rain," he said in that dead voice of his. Lightning screamed across the skies above them, and its answering thunder crashed around them as if to make it clear how bad the weather was. "There are several others before yours."

So, if the rains and winds continued unabated, there would be deep mud and ruts filling each lane of the lists. The baron's men could try to smooth them out between challenges, but they would not interfere between each run with the lances. Strategies filled his thoughts as he ate some bread and cheese to break his fast.

He'd fought in rain and mud before. 'Twasn't easy on man or beast, but he'd done it. He stared at the flap of the tent whipping in the winds and considered what to do.

"Martel, go and speak to the knights I am to face. I do not wish to sacrifice the horses in this storm to give them a chance to fight me. Increase the gold offered if 'tis too dangerous for the horses, and we meet only on the ground."

"Sir," Martel began. Thomas shook his head and waved off anything else he would say.

"They are not stupid, Martel. Their mounts must live to fight another day and are not easily replaced in their situations." He knew, because Martel had told him, that the two men were not wealthy and had barely scraped together gold enough to be taken seriously in a challenge. "Appeal to their common sense or their purses, whichever you think best. If the conditions warrant this and they refuse, make certain they know the king has sent several other horses for my use."

He could see that the king's man wanted to argue with him. But the winds suddenly tore the tent flap free and sent it flying through the camp. Any argument was forestalled until that could be handled, and then Thomas turned his attention to his armor, ignoring the man. From Martel's lack of mirth, Thomas was certain Martel had seen the logic in his offer, for there was no reason to risk laming and then needing to destroy a valuable asset for their masters' lack of sense.

But, Martel was unsuccessful in his attempts after all. So, as arranged, once finished with the long process of lining up and parading with the other knights and then being called to fight by the baron's marshal, he did indeed meet both his opponents on horseback first and then finished on the ground

He was caked with mud—on and under his armor and mail, as well as under his helm and in what hair he had— and had to change his surcoat between opponents. In spite of having superior skills with sword and staff and feeling confident of his ability to defeat both of these knights, the day's fights did not go as he'd planned.

Not at all.

When he reached his tent after fighting the two, Thomas knew he had won by luck and that his reputation and skills had served him not this day. Oh, he could blame it on the weather—which was a legitimate reason—but he knew he had fought with a lack of his usual grace and prowess. He could not seem to keep his feet under him, sliding about in the almost ankle-deep mud as if he were ten cups in on a night of heavy drinking.

Now, covered in the muck that did not come off when his armor did, Thomas stood in his tent, trying to avoid the truth about today and the morrow. After placing two large buckets of hot water in the corner, Martel left the tent. However, he had taken the opportunity to give Thomas the most disgraceful sneer that Thomas had ever seen given by someone who was not royalty.

Exhausted, sore as hell, and disturbed, Thomas let it go with only an order to leave him alone. He began stripping off his quilted hauberk, undertunic and chausses and breeches as he moved towards the steaming water. His shoulders ached from the blows delivered to his armor and absorbed by his body. He'd allowed too many strikes past his shield. So many things had gone wrong in both fights. So many mistakes. And looking up to see le Govic and Annora's father watching with glee as he went down over and over had not helped.

The abuse he'd taken today would haunt him on the morrow when le Govic would be relentless. Having observed the fights, he would strike at the places where Thomas had been hit most today. He shuddered for a moment and dipped the washing cloth into the bucket.

He washed his body and then rinsed the mud from his head and hair, all the time trying to come up with a way to plan his method of attack for tomorrow's fight. As he stood and poured the final bit of water over his head and then sluiced it down over his body, footsteps behind him warned him of a visitor.

"Martel, I told you to go. Get out now," he yelled sharply, surprising even himself that he managed to give an order at all.

"I will leave if you insist. But I would prefer to stay."

Even if he had little strength, even if he did not wish to face her criticism of today's fights, even if he needed time alone to sort his plans for the morrow, the astounded expression on her face when he turned towards her convinced him to relent. For he was completely naked, and she was staring once more at his cock and seeing it clearly. His flesh did an admirable job of rising in her presence, no matter his exhaustion.

"Then, you should stay, my lady."

She suspected that it was normal for a large man to have a large...appendage, so Annora should not be so surprised by the truth of it there before her. As Thomas turned and discovered she had trespassed on his privacy, his flesh rose out of the dark curls between his legs, and its length was enough to reach his waist. She'd seen some of him the other night when she'd spied on him, but this view of his attributes was interesting and thrilling and scary and exciting all at once.

Her mouth dried, her hands itched to touch him to test the hardness of his body, all of it, and hers ached for everything he'd promised to do, even while knowing she did not understand all of it. He wore nothing but that smile—the dangerously attractive one that dared her to wickedness—and he made no move to cover himself because of her appearance there in his tent.

"What brings you here in the dark of night, *again*, my lady?" he asked as he took a step towards her.

This brought him out of the shadows and into the light given off by the lanterns spread around the tent. She inhaled swiftly as her view of him was enhanced by the flickering flames. Her gaze could not resist the sight of his manhood there before her on display. With him naked already, her purpose here this night might be easier after all. Annora blinked several times and met his gaze.

"I but thought you might need someone to put that liniment you spoke of on your new bruises." She tugged her cloak off her shoulders to expose her own—now much darker and etched in colors—to him. Pushing her braided hair over her shoulder so it would not block his view, she shrugged. "We match now."

When he stepped fully into the light, she saw how wrong she was about that. She'd seen men fight before and thought she knew how punishing the blows could be, but facing him now, her stomach clenched at the sight of the bruises blooming on him. The worst was on his shoulders and ribs. A large one on his leg.

"Oh, Thomas," she whispered as she stepped closer to him and reached out to touch his skin. "Do they hurt as much as I think they must?"

His breathing stopped at the first touch of her fingers. She slid them down gently, outlining the edge of the bruise on his ribs. Although he did not move beneath her exploration, his flesh reacted between them. Annora wanted to touch him there, but these injuries needed attention.

"Where is that liniment you spoke of? Would it help these?" she asked, already looking around the tent for a trunk or place he'd have stored it.

"Liniment?" he asked.

His voice was rough and shaky. She glanced at his face and noticed he panted now, as though just done running a great distance. So, he was not unaffected, no matter his extensive experience in such matters? A surge of confidence and boldness filled her then. Aye, she was innocent and a maiden, but she was curious and very much in need of Thomas's help. First, though, she would aid him.

"The liniment for my injuries," she said, pointing at her neck. "The one you said your sainted mother would be horrified you offered to me?"

He smiled then and nodded. "In my trunk," he said.

"Why do you not fetch it, and I can apply it for you? Surely, you cannot reach these areas on your back and shoulders."

She skimmed her fingers up and over those broad shoulders and down, leaning around him to reach. His body lurched then, and she nearly grabbed hold of what she could to keep her balance until he took her by her shoulders and moved her a few steps farther away from him.

This was how flirting felt? This was how women had power? Seduction could work both ways, even if her aunt and others had made it seem like a dark and perilous thing men did to women. Nay, 'twas not just for men. Her body shivered with the heat that spread as she thought of the possibilities that could happen between them if she took the first step.

Annora noticed he pulled a garment out of the trunk when he searched for the liniment. Before he turned back to her, he'd tugged a pair of loose breeches up over his legs and tied them at his hips. She smiled as she saw the fabric pushed up by his hardened flesh.

And that was her plan, was it not? To come here, to commiserate with him over the difficult challenges of the day and to boost his spirits about facing le Govic? And to advise him as she could to aid him in his battle.

Oh, and to ask him to relieve her of her maidenhead so that le Govic had no chance of taking it.

Annora would hate to do it, but she could not ignore that though Thomas had won the battles this morn, it had been a near thing both times. And those ugly and unsatisfactory victories would weigh heavy on his mind and could interfere with his strategy of winning against his next opponent. She swallowed, trying to loosen the tightness in her throat that happened every time she thought about belonging to le Govic. Nay, she would not think on that right now, not while this matter was at hand.

Thomas held out the small covered bowl to her, and in the moment before she touched it, it felt like he was offering her more than this unguent to apply. His gaze softened and he looked more approachable, more touchable than he had before.

Her eyes lowered to that ever-present hardness that his breeches did not disguise. Though his expression did not speak of seduction, his flesh was clearly inviting her closer. How could she see that and not want to wrap her hands around it and slide them along its length?

"Annora, you're staring at my cock again," he whispered.

"I...'Tis just that I..." She swallowed again and reached out, passing his extended hand to lay hers on the ridge pushing against the fabric. "I am curious," she admitted. Meeting his eyes, she smiled. Ever since she'd witnessed that woman laying her hands on him, she'd wanted to know how he felt.

"You will kill me, lass."

Annora pulled her hand away, shaking her head. Had she hurt him there? He chuckled then and drew her hand back in place, even guiding her fingers to slide lower, under his cock to touch him more intimately.

"And 'twill be a happy death at that," he said. He leaned against her hand more fully while he put the bowl down. His flesh surged against her palm, lengthening and growing harder.

"But your bruises need attention." When she would have removed both of her hands, he held them there.

"*I* need attention." He did something with his hips that

thrust him against her hands. From his low moan, it must have been pleasurable. He repeated it once, then twice, and she clung tighter as he moved.

The core of her, and the place between her own legs, grew achy and hot as she stroked him. Thomas stood unmoving in the silence, his heavy breathing the only sound, and permitted her to do as she wished. Would he allow her to untie the laces and slip her hands within? Just as she lifted one hand to tug open his breeches, he took a deep breath and stepped away.

"Why are you here, Annora? You said to offer me help. Then you stoke my desire for you for your curiosity. If you persist, this is going to end with you beneath me on that pallet. So mayhap this is a good time for you to go."

Annora dropped her hands to her side and let out a loud sigh. Then frustration and anger built within her, pushing to be released.

"I do not understand you," she said. "Every time we have met, even that first time at Prudhoe, you have attempted to seduce me. You have touched me in ways that are inappropriate for two people such as us. You have kissed me until my thoughts and wits scatter in the breeze. You have made me want to touch and kiss and...handle you in ways I had never thought about until I met you." She clenched her hands into fists then. "And now, I stand here offering you my virtue, and you play the coy one?"

"What in the hell, Annora?" he yelled in a manner not unlike that day in the marketplace. "What are you thinking? Why would you do such a thing with a man like me?"

He began that strange talking that he'd done before—cursing and speaking but doing it almost silently, so she could only hear every few words. Particularly the vulgar ones, and she did not stop him. Most people never spoke that way in front of ladies. Then he stopped suddenly and stared at her as though he'd only just recognized who she was.

"You do not think I will win."

Annora blinked several times and tilted her head, studying him. The truth or a prevarication? The truth.

"I watched you fight for the first time today and have little other upon which to base my judgement. And my expectations." The words sounded terrible, even to her own ears.

"You think I will lose." He let out a loud growl. "So, this, *this*," he motioned with his hand between their bodies, "is an offer to rut with me out of pity?"

"Nay!" she cried out. The shock of the words passed, and she thought on it. "Well, mayhap?" When his eyes widened, she nodded. "Aye." Only the song of crickets and the occasional shout or two outside in the area of the tents could be heard as she waited.

"The women at Prudhoe said that men liked to indulge in pleasurable pursuits before fighting and then afterwards to spend their excitedness and vigor. Is that not true?"

He did it again then—he laughed. The sound of it caused an inexplicable tremor in her. Her body reacted to the way his face changed and how his whole body let go. Familiar with the way he looked when in charge or when he was the one intent on seduction, Annora understood this was the other side of him that many did not see. Or mayhap had not seen in a very long time? That thought made her want to weep. For he looked alive now as his shoulders shook with it and his eyes filled with tears from the strength of his chortling. He rubbed his eyes with the heels of his hands and met her gaze.

"Well, those women know of what they speak. But, lass, right or wrong, I accept your offer."

"But your shoulders? I just realized I've not applied the liniment to—"

"Fuck the liniment, Annora." At her gasp, he smiled that wicked smile that melted her insides and made her willing to do anything with him. "Lay with me, Annora. Now?"

At that moment, she understood that joining with him would be filled with laughter and epithets and passion and pleasure—all things that would never be with...

And she wanted to know this, know him, before the real world, and its consequences intruded once more.

"Aye, now."

Fourteen

He did not care if she fucked him for pity's sake.

He did not care if she thought he would lose tomorrow's challenge.

And he could not care less if she were just interested in joining with him because of her damnable curiosity.

Thomas knew before he asked her that if she consented, he would take her to that pallet next to them and show her pleasure that would have her moaning and begging for more. No matter the reason for it, or the reasons against it that he was trying to ignore.

And then she said, "aye."

His randy cock rose without delay, though in truth, it had never truly relaxed from the moment she'd entered his tent. When he reached down and tugged the laces of his breeches loose, her eyes grew wide, and the color of them resembled the line between the sky and sea on a stormy day.

Thomas watched as a parade of emotions flitted across her blushing face. She was so expressive and did not seem embarrassed about her curiosity and her own desires. In that single moment, before he moved or she did, he wondered if he would get out this unscathed.

The breeches slipped from his hips, and he watched as

her gaze tracked every inch of their journey to the ground. When he recognized only interest there, and as he watched a becoming blush creeping into her cheeks, he reached down and touched himself, grasping his cock in one hand the way he liked it and sliding it down and up his length. Annora's beautiful mouth dropped open, and her body trembled as he continued to pleasure his own flesh.

"I would rather not be the only naked one, Annora. Remove your gown for me," he urged. He would like nothing more than to stroke his flesh as he watched his fantasy come to life before his eyes.

"I must be naked as well?" she asked. Did she realize that her nipples had hardened to peaks, ones he'd felt before and now wanted to suckle until she screamed? Even now, as her hands slid down over the gown she'd questioned removing, her body was ripening. Blooming.

"I could toss your gown up and take you from behind, but being naked offers so many more pleasures." He said it, and her body shivered once more. He took a step closer. "You do want me to pleasure you, do you not, Annora?"

Her fingers flew to her own laces—ones along the sides of her gown, which she could manage, and then up to the ones that tied the back of her gown shut, which she could not. A cry of frustration echoed around them.

"Here now, sweetling," he whispered, turning her around to face away. "Let me help."

Thomas leaned down, tugged her braid out of his way and kissed his way along her spine, as he loosened the ties inch by inch. He felt every tremor rushing through her against his mouth and let his heated breath warm and tease her skin, now separate from his mouth by only a thin shift of nearly transparent linen. 'Twould not be long before that was removed.

But the fine fabric need not be a deterrent at all, as he showed her then. Easing his hands inside her gown, he pushed that off her shoulders as he eased his way behind her. When he pushed it down over her hips, his hands followed. He cupped her mound even as pressed his prick against her arse. Her breathing stopped briefly before returning in shallow gasps.

"You see now? This is how your hands felt on my flesh. As you stroked me down to my sac." He kept his fingers together and slid his hand over the curls he could feel through her shift and into the place between her legs. It took but three strokes before she opened her legs and let him go farther. "Do you like it, Annora? You must say so or I need stop." He did pause then, his hand between her thighs and growing wet with her arousal.

Deeper would come soon, and it—she—would be glorious to watch.

Her head thrashed now against his shoulder where she'd let it fall and, only when he stopped completely, did she moan out a word. It may have been "aye" or something else, but it was not "nay." So, he pressed the heel of his hand harder against her curls and let his fingers separate and find their way. As he knew would happen, the linen was not a barrier for, indeed, it provided a bit of friction that teased her onward.

Devil that he was, he whispered in her ear then. "May I kiss you there, Annora? Your juices will be so sweet on my tongue." Her legs clenched around his hand, and she shuddered, so close to satisfaction that he was not certain she had not reached it.

"You can do such a thing?" she asked in a throaty voice that made him weak with desire.

"Oh, aye. That, and so much more." He slipped his hand out and followed the curve of her belly up to her breasts. Cupping them, he rubbed his thumbs over their tips until she wriggled against him again. "So much more. But right now, I want my mouth there."

As he said the words, he began to gather the length of

her shift in his hands and tug it higher and higher. Because of his height, he could look over her shoulder and watch as every succulent inch of her was exposed. When the shift reached her waist, he turned her to face him and pulled it up and over her arms and head and tossed it aside.

God Almighty, she was magnificent! As he'd suspected, her body was perfection in its feminine curves and the lushness of her breasts. Her skin was like the pale white of the sands on those beaches in the north of Scotland. Her breasts filled his hands when he held them, and their tips were the color of roses in spring—deepest pink—and tight like buds waiting to be teased to bloom fully. The curls between her legs mirrored the golden shades of her long hair.

But it was her face and the incandescent expression in her eyes that threatened his control. She watched him with wonder as she reveled in the pleasure that he gave with just his hands. Thomas reached over and did something he'd wanted to since the day they'd met—he pulled the tie from her braid and threaded his hands into her hair, shaking it loose until it fell in waves over her body and almost to the floor.

Then, he stepped a pace back and just stared at her while touching himself. When she stepped closer and reached out towards his flesh, he shook his head.

"Nay?" she asked in a shaky voice. "I may not touch you?"

"If you touch me now, this will end in a very quick resolution," he said as he tugged on his erection. "Why not touch yourself, and I will watch you?"

"Thomas!" she exclaimed. Her innocence was refreshing and beguiling at once.

"Have you never done that? Never ached there and satisfied it?"

What thing to ask her! And what a topic of discussion to have, naked and facing a well-endowed rampantly erect man for the first time! He had teased her body and now tempted her mind with erotic thoughts and offerings. The man was a devil in the flesh. And what flesh it was!

When she hesitated to do as he'd suggested, more because she had no idea of how to begin than being opposed to it, he opened his arms to her...and she walked right into his embrace. The heat of his skin against hers forced the breath from her body. To feel the differences between them—soft and hard, tall and short, all angles against so many curves—caused a throbbing beat within her private place where he'd wanted her to touch herself.

Before she knew what he was about, he wrapped his arms around her waist and drew her up in his arms. When he guided her legs to encircle his body, she felt the hard length of him glide along her woman's flesh. Holding her up with his hands beneath her legs, he rubbed himself there, sliding in the wetness her body made.

"This will ease my way inside you, Annora," he promised as he thrust along her. She wrapped her arms around his shoulders and held on, barely in control enough to keep herself from falling. But he did. He kept her there, rocking her as he built a marvelous tension within her body. "I still want to kiss you there. Let me?"

She took his mouth then, wanting to taste his tongue and feel it against hers. Swirling and dipping in, he tasted her, thrusting in as his cock moved in the same motion along her flesh. Then, when she could not breathe or speak or do anything by dint of will, he walked them over and knelt on the pallet, easing her back until she lay there. He lifted his mouth from hers and began to kiss and lick...and nip his way down her body.

Her body arched off the pallet when he drew the tip of her breast into his mouth. His teeth replaced his lips, and she grabbed his head, his still short hair was not enough to take hold of, both pulling him away and pulling him closer every other moment. 'Twas so much, too much. Too many sensations racing through her, burning under her skin, and rushing through her blood. And within moments, her body melted and fell apart. Wave after wave of pleasure, of tightening and release, moved through her, into her, around her, and her body shuddered as it did.

"Oh God, Annora!" he whispered against her skin. "You are glorious in finding your satisfaction."

She did not know what he meant, but when he placed his palm against her curls, she arched against it as the pleasure coursed once more. Several more times, her body tightened within her core and then exploded in a torrent of feelings that filled her. She opened her eyes and discovered him leaning over her, staring at her.

"What happened?" she asked. Oh, her aunt and others had told her about joining with a man. She had witnessed various parts of it during her life, but no one had told her there was pleasure to be had simply from the touch of a hand or mouth...or tongue. And teeth? She shivered then, and he laughed and shifted closer. From the press of his cock against her leg, she could tell he had not finished.

"A miracle, truly," he said. "You allowed me to pleasure you."

"No one told me about this part," she said. "They warned me not to be taken or let a man put his...inside me. They never told me about this part." Partly she was disgruntled about not knowing, and partly, she just did not care now that she'd discovered it.

"That," he said, leaning in for a quick kiss, "is because if you'd known, you would seek it out relentlessly."

Only then did she realize that his hand was still on, in, the curls between her legs. When she shifted, and one finger slipped between the folds of her flesh, she moaned.

"Too much?" he asked.

"Not enough, I think," she murmured. "Show me more."

His laughter at her bold demand warmed her heart. There would be time later for regrets or sadness. For now, she would take of whatever pleasure or satisfaction he offered and keep them in her heart for those darker times she was certain were ahead.

He kissed her swiftly and then climbed up over her, moving down her body again but this time not stopping at her breasts. Oh, he kissed them and suckled them and then lowered himself along her. She'd been ticklish as a child and thought she would giggle when he reached her belly. A moan escaped instead at his intimate touch and she lifted her head to watch him and did whatever he told her to do.

So, when he'd spread her legs and laid between himself them, she found herself unable to do anything but feel as she saw him kiss and lick closer and closer to that aching place. He slid his hands under her legs then, took hold of her thighs and pulled her against his mouth.

His mouth.

His lips.

His tongue.

Oh, dear God, his tongue! The first warning was no warning at all, but a long slide along the flesh there. From deep between her legs, along the throbbing folds until he reached...something...some place that needed to be touched. His tongue just teased around that place, a place she'd never known had existed until him, until now. Until his tongue pressed it and touched it and tasted her...there!

Every feeling in her body centered there, beneath his tongue. Then he pushed in and took the small bit of her flesh into his mouth and did what he'd done on her breasts, and she fell back, moaning. Her hands slid down and covered her breasts that ached almost painfully so, and his movements grew harder and faster. Her hips rose to meet his mouth, faster and faster until he slid back away from the tormented place. Annora pushed up on her elbows to watch him again.

His eyes were focused on her intimate place, as though single-minded in finding whatever he wanted there. When she felt his tongue thrust deeper, she was stunned to feel him push within her folds and even within her body. How could she feel him there? Her body craved him, it hungered, wanting *something,* and she knew he would give it to her.

"Thomas!" she whispered out. She reached out for him, wanting to take hold of something, but she could only touch his head. "I need..."

"More, sweetling? Did you beg for *this*?" When he laughed this time, her flesh felt the vibration of it, and she tensed there. "Oh no, you do not," he warned.

But it made no sense to her until she spun once again out of control. Her body shuddered over and over as she fell apart beneath his sensual onslaught. Just when she thought she was gaining some sense of herself, his teeth grazed over a place that was so sensitive, so aching that it almost hurt. Until he licked it. Her hips canted, and he used his teeth again. Annora grabbed his head and held him there, thrusting her hips against his mouth as he'd done against her palms. That laugh excited her flesh yet again until she thought she could take not bear it.

Her body wound tighter and tighter only to explode into pieces when he suckled that one spot. He was as relentless in his attentions now as his pursuit had been, and Annora found herself floating, her body satiated and throbbing. Then, when she could breathe, he lifted his head up, exposing her heated folds to the coolness of the tent.

She cried out, but within the passing of only a moment or two, he covered her body, and she felt his cock there where his tongue had been. As he kissed her mouth, bracing himself on his elbows, she could taste the essence of her arousal on his mouth.

"I told you it would taste sweet," he whispered.

He watched her eyes as his flesh pressed a scant bit into her folds. She knew how big he was. She knew how hard he was. But, as he slid slowly in, Annora realized that his motions felt good. He paused then, and she tightened the muscles within her so she could feel him.

"You little witch," he said, kissing her hard. "Lift your hips, sweetling. Now."

She did, and he thrust deep, entering her in one swift movement and filling her and taking her maidenhead. Her flesh burned and felt very stretched there, and yet it did not hurt as she'd imagined it would.

"That was not bad," she said.

He lifted his head and shook it. "Not bad, Annora?"

"I expected more pain," she explained. "From your size," she felt his cock harden more within her, "I did not think it would be that easy." This time his laughter was like a rumble of thunder that came from deep in his chest. "Are we done then?"

Instead of answering her, Thomas withdrew himself a bit. When she thought he would leave her completely, he slowly thrust back in, deeper than he had been.

"Oh." Her body awakened a little. When he withdrew, her hips followed him, and she moaned this time when he thrust all the way in. "Oh."

"Aye," he whispered back as he pulled out and then plunged back in, deeper with each thrust. "We are not done, lass."

Her body, it seemed, was not either, for her skin, her muscles, her flesh all woke until his attentions, and when he filled her with his flesh and began to moan, she took him in and tightened around him then. He gasped with each movement now, and she felt his seed spill into her. Clenching around him, the throbbing of his flesh brought on his release within her and let herself sink into it with him.

Although he remained within her, Annora grew aware

when his breaths grew even, and she waited. Her body felt used and exposed and...wonderful. It was not as she'd imagined it would be and yet, so much more. Though there would be regrets later. For now, she reveled in the feeling of complete satisfaction under his warm body.

He shifted to one side and held his weight off of her, allowing her to breathe easier. As he did, he glanced down her body and up to her face.

"Are you well, lass?" he asked. A bit embarrassed by this strange intimacy, she nodded.

Would she ever act or reply or respond as he expected of her?

Thomas could do nothing but laugh at the words she'd uttered in reviewing their joining. He'd exerted an unbelievable amount of restraint in bedding her, knowing it was her first time, and her reaction was he'd not done badly? Men feared him. Women adored him. And Annora thought he wasn't bad.

Though the words could be an insult in another time or with another person, he took them for nothing less than her innocent, honest assessment of their experience. Just as she did in almost every encounter, she did or said the most unexpected thing, and his heart almost felt alive once more from her candor. It had been so long since he had been able to trust anyone and believe that their word was true.

And here, his enemy's daughter was the one, inviting him to seek a path other than the one he'd chosen for himself. To look in a different direction from the one he'd thought could be his only way.

Yet, he knew he could not, and it saddened him.

Oh, she had not come here seeking more than the pleasure they'd shared, and he'd made certain she had gotten that in full measure. So, if she was satisfied in their exchange, why was he not?

"I am well, considering," she said. When he nudged her to continue, she said, "When I woke and broke my fast in the lord's hall, I had no expectation that, by nightfall, I would be a fallen woman." She shook her head then and he eased out of her. "Lady Clara would be thunderstruck by this turn in things."

"Lady Clara?"

"Oh, one of the noblewomen here. I think she may be from Normandy. Her mother seeks a marriage for her. I met her this morn when Lord Yves invited me to the morning meal there. We walked to the fields together."

"And you told Lady Clara about me?" His pleasure in that lasted only moments until she dragged him down.

"Oh, nay! I would never speak to a stranger about our...arrangement. Though it would be nice to have a friend with whom I could discuss private matters."

From what he knew of her, Annora lived with her father, and her only living relative was her late mother's older sister. Someone as lively and as young as she should have many friends and attendants. She had no siblings. Before he could ask a question, she turned on her side and met his gaze.

"So, what happens now?"

"Now?"

"Are we finished?" she asked. A shy glance down and then back to his face reminded him once more of her inexperience. "I thought we had finished before, but I was wrong." She shifted to lie on her side and face him. "Is there more, or should I go?"

He noticed a lack of confidence in her words he'd not heard before. This was unknown territory for her—having never been bedded before and now facing the one who'd taken her virginity. If he admitted the truth of how things had progressed, it was more a situation of she'd *given* it to him, yet that mattered not. Thomas had been the first man to touch her or kiss her or possess her body. Realizing then he'd been lost in his thoughts and had not answered her question, he shook his head.

"The part where we join is finished, Annora. If it is safe for you to stay, I pray you will." When she frowned at his words, he closed the space between them and kissed her swollen lips softly. "Will your father be looking for you?"

"He and," her face took on an expression of disgust before she said the name, "le Govic were celebrating over with the..." He nodded, understanding where they were now. "Father is deep in some intrigue and pays me little heed except when he wants me to be someplace or another." She inhaled and released a shaky breath. "Do you know of the matter?"

A tremor of unease passed through him then. A reminder that this endeavor, so to speak, between them, had much larger influences than his or le Govic's skills in the fight on the morrow. When kings and princes ran amuck, sticking their greedy, prideful fingers everywhere, no simple fight was that simple. And Thomas neither trusted or fully believed his king or the English prince to be forthright in this arrangement.

"I know only my part in it, Annora. The king dragged my arse from his dungeon and offered me all I'd lost if I fought in this challenge. It did not take me long to agree without asking for his reasons. When you are caught somehow between a king and a prince, 'tis best to keep your head low enough to avoid having it taken off." He slid his arm up and rested his head on his hand, watching her. "The thing I do not understand, and that puzzles me the most, though, is why would your father risk Prudhoe and you to accept this challenge?"

He sat up then and grabbed a blanket to toss over them.

The chill in the night air raised gooseflesh on his skin and, he noticed, on hers. "That is the part that makes no sense to me."

"I know not," she said. She slid down to be completely under the cover of the blanket. He tucked it around her. "Only messages from the king's brother and then you arrived. Father ranted for hours after you left that day." She laughed then before going on. Rolling onto her back, she nodded at him. "I thought he was having an apoplectic fit. 'Twas only days, or a sennight later, that I learned about this tournament and this private challenge that I was to be given away as part of the prize."

"So, we are both puppets to be strung up and played as these royals desire?" He let out a frustrated groan. "I suspect they pit both sides against themselves as well as the other. We will lose no matter who wins tomorrow's challenge."

He'd suspected that from the first—that there would be no winner in this matter unless it was a king or prince. And those two hatched plots for their own private and nefarious reasons, known only to them.

"'Tis clear to me that my father looks to the prince for something that our king will not give him. Could it be the same for your king?"

"Beholden to Prince John?" He shrugged. "With these royals, anything is possible. I am certain of one thing," he said. "This goes back years in its scope. Decades to when William originally lost Northumberland to the old king, Henry. What happened back then is what is driving this matter now. Of that, and only that, I am certain."

When a yawn escaped her, he realized that Annora was as exhausted as he was. The lull in vitality that followed finding satisfaction in the body of a woman always made him want to sleep. But first, he must see to her. Climbing off the pallet, he sought out the bucket, finding no water there. The cloth was damp yet, so he took it and with a bit of water in his jug, handed it to Annora. The puzzlement on her face again demonstrated her innocence.

"To...to use to...clean..." It turned out he might know what needed to be done but could not explain it to the temptress who sat on his bed, gathering her hair into a rough braid. When she stopped in the middle of weaving the sections together and stared at him, Thomas knew she'd understood. Grabbing up his garments, he turned his back to her as he dressed in the breeches and tunic and pulled on shoes, so that he could escort her back.

He faced her and found her in her gown, waiting for him to tie the back laces. The urge to pull it off once more filled him, and he fought it off, knowing that there was no time for such things and that she would be sore from his attentions so far. But after she healed and after he won on the morrow...

"You will be the victor, Thomas."

"Can you read my thoughts now?" She faced away from him, so she could not see a sign of his lack of confidence revealed on his face.

"I felt you stiffen just then. I suspected that the morrow had infringed on this evening." Crossing her arms over her chest, she examined him in a brisk look from head to his toes. "How am I to apply the liniment if you are garbed? Take it off, Thomas." His body reacted as it should to a command such as that one—his flesh rose, awaiting what it hoped would come next.

"Does...*it* always do that?"

"When you look at *it* or speak of *it*, aye, *it* does," he said. With one glance at her face then, Thomas knew he was falling in love with this extraordinary woman. But he could not think about that now. "So, turn your gaze away, woman!" he teased.

"Thomas, I am not leaving until you allow me to help

you," she said, retrieving the bowl and removing the tight-fitting lid. The obnoxious scent of it filled the tent. "By all the saints, this smells just like..."

"Shite?" he answered. "I am certain there is manure in it for it to smell as it does. I was trying to spare your sensibilities."

"Too late," she said. Her face tightened in an expression of revulsion as she dipped her fingers in the unguent and held it up. "I truly hope this is helpful. To suffer such a smell for nothing would be pitiful." He tugged off the tunic and turned his back to her first. "You said your mother would be horrified but never explained why. Now I know."

She worked in companionable silence then, scooping, spreading and working the mixture into the skin on the worst of the bruising. He would appreciate it on the morrow, he knew. She moved around to put it on his ribs, and every few moments, she would chuckle, and he knew she was watching his randy flesh throb against his breeches.

"I will win," he whispered to her.

"I expect you to live up to your part of our bargain, Sir Thomas," she said, wiping the last of the medicament off her hands with a cloth he held out. "I do not wish to suffer the attentions of that man again for even a moment."

"Very well, my lady," he said, lowering his head in a curt bow.

"Do you know how you will defeat him?" Leave it to her to cut through the flowery promise to its core—an oath with no plan.

"Fight like the devil and take advantage of a weakness?" He lifted her cloak, shook it out and tossed it around her shoulders. She tucked her braid under the collar and pulled the hood up around her head.

"And that weakness is?" She met his gaze, and hers

narrowed. "I am inexperienced at such matters, but he did not seem to reveal such a weakness in his battles yesterday."

"Nay, he did not." Thomas thought on what he'd witnessed and the changes in both of them over the years since he'd fought the man last. "He tended to rely on his size to intimidate. On a horse, with a lance aimed at your chest, size like his, and mine, can be a disadvantage."

"What else?" she asked. "You are both rather big men. Does that balance out the threat of being large in breadth and height?"

He shook his head and blinked to clear his vision. Thomas had underestimated Annora and she'd shown him the folly of such an act as she demonstrated her ability to dissect a problem or situation. Which made him realize there were ways to use both his size and le Govic's against him in their fight.

"Aye, it could. Or I could use it, knowing how well matched we are in that. The only good thing about today's challenges is that he did not see my best to judge me by. He saw me at my worst, so he will not expect much in the fight tomorrow. Take him unawares."

He gathered her in his arms and spun them around in circles, holding her up until he could kiss her. And he did—again and again until he grew dizzy, and she grew breathless.

"I will fight for you," he said when he placed her before him. "I want you, Annora. I want my lands and title back, but I want you for..."

He stopped before he could utter the words. She stared at his mouth, waiting for the rest of it. Did she know that his original plan was changing with every moment spent with her? With every new facet he saw of her person and the woman she was...and the wife she could be?

Thomas was not certain of anything at all. So many

depended on his restoration that throwing any part of that away or discounting the importance of each part—including needing a well-connected noble *Scots* wife—seemed foolhardy. Now was not the time to announce his feelings to her, other than the one she was well aware of, or to proclaim he wanted to wed her. All of that must wait until he carried out the first crucial step—beat le Govic.

"Come, 'tis time to go," he said, holding out his hand to her.

She took his hand but tugged on him to stop. "There is something else," she said, shaking her head and shrugging as she spoke.

"Are you well? Is there discomfort? Tell me true, Annora—did I hurt you?" He had not inquired enough about her condition after their encounter.

"'Tis not about that, and aye, I am well," she said. Did she notice that she slid her hand in his as she spoke? "There is something about him. Something strange. He seems to favor his right side."

"He is right-handed, Annora, as are most," he said.

"Nay, 'tis something else I noticed. Not on the lists. Before. Outside of fighting. I cannot sort it out, but I will."

"Before the battle on the morrow?" he asked. She looked ready to slap him, so he leaned in for a kiss instead.

"I will send word when I make sense of it."

Thomas gathered her hand back in his and began to lead her out of the tent when she stopped yet another time. She searched within her cloak for something, and the smile that lit her face spoke of success.

"I cannot give you this on the morrow," she said, holding out her hand that curled in a fist. "I wanted you to know that you have my favor, and I will be praying for your success."

She relaxed her fingers, and a cloud of silk dropped into his palm, waiting beneath her hand. He did as he had with each one that he'd stolen without her knowledge—he gathered it together and inhaled the scent of her that remained in the delicate swath of silk.

"I thank you for this, Annora."

Tears filled her eyes, and she ducked her head lower to keep him from seeing them. This time she led the way out, and they skirted around the tents, keeping to the shadows until they were closer to her father's. He released her hand and waited for her to cross the last short distance alone, stepping back into the darkness to cover his presence. Just before she turned to enter, she crossed back towards him. He saw the tears streaming down her cheeks now and wanted to take her away, steal her, keep her safe. Keep her as his own.

"I just want you to know, Thomas. I wanted it to be you. I so wanted it to be you."

And then she disappeared, running to the tent and entering quietly.

Sixteen

As she opened her eyes in the morning, Annora was glad that this morn was as bright as yesterday's had been gloomy. She did not rise immediately; instead, she allowed herself to adjust to her new condition of being.

A woman, no longer a child.

A woman, no longer chaste.

A woman, in love with a man.

She sensed that her life might be easier if none of those things were true, but they were, and she would live with the choices she'd made. Except for falling in love—that had happened without her even trying. But if she never spoke of it and did not admit to it, it could all be well.

When Annora shifted under the thick layers of bedclothes, her body reminded her of what had changed. She had allowed, nay opened herself and invited, a man into her body. She had touched him and kissed him, and he had filled her in a place she'd not known was empty. His consideration and attention and care of her tore down her defenses, leaving her raw in spirit and heart. Her body he had cherished, and other than a twinge in a few deep places, she felt alive and filled with vigor and ready for more.

When she told him that she'd wanted it to be him, it

was the true reason she'd sought him out. At first, he was the lesser of the two terrible possibilities before her. She hated her father for putting her in the middle of this devil's bargain, one that she would lose no matter who won.

That was before Thomas began his planned attack on her.

Not one meant to harm her, but one meant to make her think and feel and question. And to use her for his purposes. Oh, she was not so naïve and stupid that she did not see his aims when they met. Beguile, frighten, tempt, test and tease.

And he'd done all of those things, making her curious and eager and willing to place herself within his sphere of influence. To present him with the opportunities to continue his seduction of her until she was ready to begin hers of him. In his need to work his wiles on her, he'd given her the freedom and power to try hers out on him.

And somewhere in all that dancing, feinting and probing, she'd seen the true man beneath his devilish façade. Under the traitor's edifice was a man of honor, one willing to allow her to believe she could take hold of her future when she was least in control. When a man of lesser honor would have taken everything from her, he'd held back until certain it was her choice. He'd let her sleep in his bed unaccosted when he could have taken her. Now, all of the preparations would conclude, and all the games would be over.

Or would they?

Something much bigger than their tiny noble but insignificant lives was at stake here. Kingdoms and loyalties were in play. Lands and titles and past wrongs waited to be restored and vindicated. Lives saved and destroyed. All lay in the balance as they awaited the outcome of a battle between two men. Puppets both. Warriors both.

As Margaret entered quietly and began gathering the garments she would wear to watch the battle that would determine the rest of her life, Annora realized she was no closer to aiding Thomas than before. She pushed back the blankets and rose to wash. Margaret's gasp at the mark on the sheet and then knowing blush told Annora her maid suspected, nay knew, the truth of where she'd gone and what she'd done.

"Do you wish a bath, my lady? I could call for the tub and hot water," she offered. But before the maid could do that, Annora's father called out her name from outside.

"I am here, Father," she said, accepting the robe Margaret offered and walking to the tent's opening. Margaret tossed the blankets back in place before her father entered.

"This is the day, Annora. The day my champion will defend our honor, and defeat an enemy of longstanding," he said, clearly pleased with himself and the proceedings.

"I did not know you were acquainted with Thomas of Kelso," she said. This was the first time her father had spoken of anything involving the cause of this, and she would discover what she could.

"Not him, stupid child," he said. "This is more important than some traitor William thinks to send my way. He did not even have the respect to send someone worthy."

"But Thomas is undefeated—" She never finished the rest, for her father struck her across the mouth and sent her stumbling back.

"Do not speak of what you do not know. None of this concerns you. You will play your part and be given to Laurence for having agreed to help me."

Annora warned Margaret off with the slightest movement of her head. The girl was usually wise but fiercely loyal and would be in danger if she attempted to protect Annora now.

"Get her dressed now," he ordered, shouting and

motioning at Margaret to heed him. "Clean up her mouth. Bring her to le Govic's tent when she is readied."

"Father?" Annora shrank back when he raised his hand, now a fist.

"You will come and watch your champion prepare for the battle. He wishes you there."

"'Tis unseemly." The words slipped out before she thought about the wisdom of speaking at all.

"Unseemly? 'Tis only unseemly if I say so and I do not. You will come and watch and be glad that you will be taken care of by such a capable man."

He was gone then, but his voice echoed back as he called out orders to his servants and le Govic's attendants. Annora looked at Margaret and recognized the dread there in her eyes.

"Oh, my lady," Margaret cried as she brought cloths and cool water to Annora's side. "Sit here and let me tend this before it swells more."

Annora fell more than sat on the chair her maid dragged over. Luckily, the bleeding was more inside her mouth than on her skin, and Margaret's skillful care had it cleaned up and her dressed in a short time. Though her legs felt as though they would not support her, Annora made her way over to le Govic's and was pulled in roughly when the tent flap was opened. Whatever she thought, she would see, 'twas not this.

Never this.

Le Govic stood surrounded by his squires, two, and other servants, three, and her father as they dressed and readied him for battle. Thankfully, they'd not waited on her arrival to begin, and he already wore chausses and a tunic. Then, the hauberk of chainmail was lifted over his head, though with his height that rivalled Thomas's, his squires had to climb on stools and benches to manage it.

Layer upon layer, cloth and mail and then armor was

placed and secured and tested to make certain it would remain where needed during the coming fights. Annora ignored most of it, lost in her thoughts as she tried to find what she was missing about him—the one weakness that would bring about his defeat this day. And, in spite of hearing stories from gathered ladies, knights or even visitors and villagers about Thomas's skills, she thought he might need something more.

Then, one of the servants whispered something to the other that drew her attention. 'Twas clear to her, they exchanged some jibe about their master, but he did not hear them. Yet, when they moved to his left side to make an adjustment in the length of the straps attached to his belt and whispered something more, he tensed and then slammed his fist into both their stomachs. They fell onto the floor and were moved aside by the others without a word.

He'd not heard them when they whispered while standing to his right side.

Could he be deaf on one side?

Good fortune was with her then, for her father went over to speak to him in low tones so that no one else would hear. Whether it was about what had just happened or some other matter, she knew not. As she watched closely, her father, who was closer and could position himself more easily on le Govic's right, moved around the massive man until he stood on his left.

Le Govic *was* deaf on his right side!

Since neither of his previous challenges had made it very far past the lances, she'd not seen him fight on the ground where movement was freer, and attacks could come from anywhere, enough to notice this. And an opponent who knew that could use it against him.

She needed to get word to Thomas before the match began. It might not help him on the list when they charged on their mounts, but on the ground, it could be useful. As she was considering how to get that knowledge to him, her father beckoned her to his side, unfortunate for it brought her to le Govic as well.

"'Tis only fitting you wish our champion well, Annora." Confused about what was expected, she waited. "A favor to give him?"

"Pray, forgive me, I left it in my trunk." Her father's eyes flashed in anger, but she called to Margaret. "Let me tell her where it is. 'Tis not one of my veils, Sir Laurence, but something special," she lied.

When her father gave her leave, she leaned close to Margaret and told her to seek out Thomas and tell him what she'd found. She sent her off running, though not on the errand the others thought.

"Annora! While we are waiting, give your champion your personal wishes." She must have shaken her head, for her father grabbed her by the arm and pulled her to the knight. "Wish your champion well. Now."

"Sir Laurence," she began, struggling to pay heed to her words when the pain from her father's harsh grasp made her sick to her stomach. She did not want to go near this brutal man, yet she could not escape. "I wish you well."

"Come closer, Annora and say the words once more." Le Govic's voice was softer and more dangerous.

Her father shoved her against le Govic, who now grabbed her head and pulled her mouth up towards his. Stretching on her toes, she fought against his grip. Keeping her in position with one hand now under her jaw, he tugged the circlet and veil free and tossed them aside. She tried to peel his fingers away, but they were clamped onto her tightly, and she had not the strength to loosen them. He dragged her mouth against hers and thrust his tongue deep inside. When she gagged, he let her go for a moment as he tore off her wimple and wrapped his arms around her to keep her still.

His mail and armor dug into her skin where it touched, and his iron hold kept her chest from pulling in air. Was she to die here? Now? He laughed at her efforts and then mauled her mouth again until she could not breathe.

"Blood? I taste blood?" he said, before shoving his tongue back in again. He maneuvered within her mouth until he could grasp her tongue with his teeth and bite it. She pushed away with all her might.

"Father?" she pleaded. When she saw that the others had gone and her father stood staring at the opening of the tent, drinking wine, she knew the knight would do as he wished to her.

"She was disrespectful, Laurence. Even today."

"Worry not, my lord," he said as he forced her face back to his. "I do not mind the taste of it on my women."

Annora realized that he relished the fight, the blood, and her resistance that was giving him. This would be her life if Thomas lost. And in that moment, as she prayed her maid would find him, Annora stopped fighting him. It took great effort, but in a very short time, the enjoyment he got from tormenting those weaker than him seeped away, and he released her.

"Bloody hell!" he yelled as he let her fall to the floor. "If you think you will lie beneath me like a lifeless fish, you had better think again. My last wife did that and see where she is now? Aye, you think about that!"

Now her father did jump up and come to them. Reaching down and helping her to her feet, her father placated him.

"Worry not, Laurence. She has her mother's spirit and stubbornness. She will be exactly what you want in a wife." The knight seemed to calm then. Her father continued, "We will sign the betrothal contracts tonight, and the marriage will be held at the feast on the morrow, after the melee."

"Betrothal this night?" she asked.

"Aye, Annora. The contract lies ready for us to sign," Le Govic said. "And we marry and leave for Normandy after the great feast."

In her pain and fear, she did not control her damnable curiosity that bothered her father so much. "But what Thom...Laurence..." She thought better of pricking an angry animal and stopped.

"It matters not, Annora. Betrothed tonight and marriage tomorrow."

"Go and fix yourself," her father said, pointing to the opening. "And make certain you bring something appropriate to give to our champion for him to carry into battle."

He walked out, and Laurence followed him but not before repeating the terrifying vow, with a new addition.

"Betrothed tonight, Annora. Wed on the morrow. And dead? We shall see."

When Margaret found her on her return, Annora sat where she'd been standing, sobbing into the torn wimple.

Thomas was now truly her only hope.

But could she trust an outlaw and traitor to do the right thing?

Seventeen

The horse sent by the king was spirited and well-trained. As Thomas sat in the line of knights awaiting to take their place before the stands, the beautiful black animal seemed to take in all the adoration of those cheering as though only for it. Thomas laughed then and gave it some head to prance as it wanted to.

This morning dawned so brightly and warm that the calamity of yesterday felt like a dream. The winds that followed the rains and the summer warmth helped to dry out most of the lanes in the lists, so they would not be filled with the sticky mud he'd faced before. Oh, there would be some spots where it had not dried, but the majority of the lists were definitely in good enough condition that it would not impede the horses or the men from getting a good foothold.

Today's field would feature several personal challenges like his with le Govic, as well as some daily challenges in the tournament itself. But the match that had gossip and rumors flying through the crowds was the one now scheduled for late in the afternoon.

A challenge to fight to the death had been issued by Sir Hugo of York to Sir Alexander de Mandeville. That Sir Hugo was so much older, and Sir Alexander was the renown fighter called the Devil's Blade added to the excitement that seemed to make everything louder and brighter. No one knew the reason behind it except the participants and Lord Yves, since he had to give leave for such a match on his lands.

He would not worry over another's match when his was still before him. Thomas's and le Govic's would not be to the death. They had agreed to do three runs with lances, and if one knight did not fall, continue to fight on the ground until one of them could not. They were not supposed to kill each other, but Thomas thought grimly that it would not stop him from trying.

Thomas paused after such dark thoughts and inhaled the sweet summer air to let it calm him. One step at a time. One fight at a time. He'd won doing that, and he would win again in that manner. In spite of not sleeping at all once Annora was safely back in her tent, he felt strong and focused and ready to do battle.

Finally, the marshal called the knights to order, and they rode along the stands and circled back to line up as they were introduced. When it was his name and le Govic's called, he guided the horse forward, ignoring how foul his opponent's mount was, and came to the center of the stands where Lord Yves sat with the guests of honor. Only then did he see Annora.

He lost control for a brief moment when he took in her pale face where a bruise was darkening the side of her cheek, and her lip was swollen. Her beautiful eyes were red, and it looked as though she had been ill or sobbing. When Lord Yves called for Lord de Umfraville to stand and accept the terms of this private challenge, Annora's father dragged her to stand.

What in the hell had happened to her?

Only when she stood, and the rays of sunlight illuminated her, did he see what she wore. And he wanted to call out her name for it.

Though her wimple was the usual white that most ladies wore, the veil covering it matched her kirtle. He was not exceedingly good at naming the colors of women's garments, but what Annora wore over her white undergown and sleeves was as close to green as cloth could be without being it. So, between the white on her head and the gown she wore, she was covered in the same colors he wore on his surcoat and on his banner.

One look at her face told him not to make any reference to it. She appeared to have been already hit or, God Almighty Forbid, beaten. Thomas would rip the one responsible into pieces for harming her. When Lord Yves asked for his assent, he nodded. Then, at le Govic's side, they crossed the few yards for the tradition of asking for their lady's favor. The silk Annora had given him last night was tucked inside, next to his heart. No matter, he must play along in this for her sake now.

"Lady Annora, do you have a favor to present to one of the knights?" asked Lord Yves.

She slipped her hand inside her sleeve and withdrew a long piece of what looked to be an expensive ribbon. He could not help the smile that sat on his face when he saw the color...green again. They both dipped their lances though they all knew how this must be done.

"I present this to you in the hope of a victory this day," she said. Did anyone else notice that, although she tied the ribbon onto le Govic's weapon, she met Thomas's gaze as if she spoke only to him?

He would not know what spurred him to boldness, but the words came out before he could consider the wisdom of engaging with her. "Nothing for me, my lady?"

He heard le Govic's growl and Lord de Umfraville's protest, but the crowd loved his nerve and roared out in support.

"Sir, you overstep," she warned him, shaking her head.

"You tell him, Annora," le Govic called out to her. "You cocky bastard," he said loud enough that Thomas heard it.

"Traitor though I may be called, bastard I am not," he replied, now raising his voice a bit, so others *did* hear his words. Then he called out again to her. "So, you have no good words for me then, my lady?"

The crowd called out many suggestions, and he laughed at some of them. Bawdy words, suggestions and advice on fighting were bandied about until the lady herself raised her hand to bring it to an end.

"Sir, you mistake yourself if you think I will be yours, for Sir Laurence has assured me that I will be betrothed to him this night and married to him on the morrow."

The crowd and le Govic roared their approval at her supportive words, but Thomas heard the threat in them. Then, though she smiled and nodded, the coldness in her gaze told him the truth of it—winner or loser, Annora would be forced to marry his opponent. He knew not how, only that her father and le Govic had a plan to bring about such a thing.

The marshal gave them leave to go to their places at the designated ends of the list, and Thomas glanced at her again as he headed to his place. Martel wait there for him. Incensed over what she'd told him in her veiled words, Thomas realized he'd seen Margaret coming to his tent earlier as he made his way to the place where the knights were called to gather.

"Martel," he beckoned the man closer. "Did Annora's maid come to my tent this morn?

"Aye, sir, I was about to tell you." Martel replied. "After you'd left, she brought word from the lady." The man waited until Thomas was ready, with his lance couched against him and then waved off the squire so no other could hear his words. "The lady believes that le Govic is deaf in his right ear. He cannot hear anything coming from that side."

"Deaf?" Thomas nodded at the words, but he was already considering how he could use it to his advantage. "I must go, Martel."

The man rushed away, and Thomas put the visor down on his helmet. As the marshal raised his hand, Thomas emptied his thoughts of everything but the man who would be hurtling towards him. Then the signal was given, and he urged his horse to a gallop.

As he rode down the lane, he adjusted the lance and aimed for a spot that would throw off his opponent's balance at the same time he shifted his seat and lowered himself to make him more difficult to hit. The hardest part of this was not flinching or moving away while aiming. The air around him seemed to still as the impact came.

The sound of wood splintering, the screams of the crowd and then the realization that he remained upright, followed in a quick procession. Turning back, he prayed he'd been successful, for le Govic had not been. His hopes were dashed when le Govic yelled out to the crowd. The two of them circled back around to their end to prepare for the next one. He was gathering up his next lance when Martel approached.

"Repeat that, if you can," he said, holding the horse's bridle to steady the horse. "It lifted him off his saddle."

Thomas nodded at the advice, for a keen observer was the best assistant a knight in the lists could have. Someone who understood the mechanics of how this worked as priceless. Mayhap he'd misjudged Martel?

"And keep your left shoulder lower," he said. "He managed to graze it that time."

And Thomas was off again, rushing towards another chance to take his opponent down. He did as Martel suggested, but he felt the blow of the lance on his shoulder even as his own crashed into le Govic's chest, knocking him free of the saddle. But would the man recover and remain astride?

When he reached the end of the run, Thomas turned to see if he was still on horseback, even as his shoulder screamed in pain from another blow to the already injured area. He shook his numb arm to regain feeling as he saw le Govic drag himself upright and remain seated.

Damn him to hell!

He tugged the reins too tightly, and his mount reared up and kicked its front legs out. Thomas struggled to control it and finally got the horse on the ground and heading back to his place. Martel came running once more and took the remnants of the lance from him, tossing it to the squire.

"You need to do it again while remaining in your own saddle," he said.

Thomas was not certain if he was being sarcastic or not. "Truly? That is the goal of this, Martel?" he asked, not needing or wanting an answer.

"Can you lean a bit more to the inside, or does it take you off your balance?"

"Nay, I cannot," he said, settling in place and gathering the lance tighter this time. He nodded at the man's suggestion. "I will try."

Sweat poured down inside his helm and into his eyes. Even the cushioning did not help that. His shoulder burned like the fires of hell, and he struggled to keep his grip of the lance. He tried to clear his thoughts in those last seconds and offered a prayer for his efforts. To save Annora.

He felt the blunt impact as his lance hit its target and lifted le Govic out of his saddle, knocking him to the ground. Thomas finished riding to the end and circled back, praying all the while that the man was down and done. Silence reigned over the lists while the marshal ran out to assess le Govic's condition. When the French words came ordering the knights to continue the fight on the ground, Thomas cursed under his breath even as he slid out of the saddle and smacked the horse's hindquarters to urge it out of the way.

Turning back as Martel took the lance and handed him his sword, Thomas knew the advantage he had right now. Yet, while le Govic was still stunned from the blow and lying on the ground, that advantage would not last long. So, armed with sword and shield, he trotted towards his opponent to get to him before the man could climb to his feet and regain his wits. He would not attack an unarmed knight, but neither would he wait until he was steady on his feet.

Le Govic was not used to being the disadvantaged one in a fight, and he struggled mightily for the few minutes. Thomas thought he might be dazed from landing as he did, but soon, the knight was gaining his bearings and fighting back. Then, Thomas was the one being thrashed under a relentless attack.

At this point in any battle, Thomas let go and stopped thinking, allowing his body to use its experience and training to carry on the fight. Instinct replaced strategy. Practice and stamina replaced the initial burst of vigor at the beginning of a battle. He had no idea how long they'd been fighting or how much longer they would—he knew only that his task was closer at hand with every blow he delivered and every one he avoided.

Then, he found an opening and aimed his sword at the left side of the knight's helm, slamming the edge of it where it was thinnest with as much strength as he could put behind it. He wanted to dent the metal while leaving le Govic disoriented. If he were unable to hear clearly in his good ear, it would give Thomas the cover he needed to approach unheard.

No amount of warnings called out by the crowds could help him either. And that blow would send waves of dizziness and make him unsteady and unable to sort out Thomas's attacks. When le Govic began clutching at the smashed helm, Thomas charged from behind the knight.

If his strength was lagging, all he did was allow a bit of his outrage over Annora's condition to replenish his resolve. He raised his sword and struck the knight one last time with the force needed to end this.

To save her. To keep her.

The next thing he heard was the screaming of the crowds. Martel reached him first and took his sword. Thomas lifted his own helm off and took a length of cloth from his squire to wipe the sweat from his eyes and his face. Though too far to see Annora clearly, he saw the gown she wore and knew she would be safe. After taking a drink of ale and a last glance as they carried le Govic from the list, Thomas followed the marshal over to the place in front of the stands where Lord Yves stood waiting for him. The baron motioned for Annora and her father to stand with him.

"You are the victor in this battle of honor, Sir Thomas of Kelso," the lord began. "Brisbois! Bone-breaker!" he called out to the crowd who began to chant his name. Lord Yves smiled, understanding and manipulating those watching. This nobleman was also clearly part monger, selling the excitement of the tournament to increase the pleasure of those attending. Regaining their attention, he said, "As the one charged with overseeing this challenge by those involved, I declare it done and decided in William of Scotland's favor." Lord de Umfraville muttered something under his breath, but Thomas cared not.

Annora was his.

He met her gaze and saw the confusion and fear still there, dimming the usual sparkle in her eyes. It would take some time for this to settle in and for them to find a way to their new life together. If she would have him, he would offer her marriage.

Annora would be his wife.

From the terrible hatred that darkened her father's face, Thomas recognized the look of a desperate man and would swear the man did not accept this outcome. As he took hold of Annora's hand and began to lead her away, Thomas knew he could not let her go with her father. What had she said before the fight?

Betrothed tonight. Wed tomorrow.

Thomas walked closer and asked to speak to Lord Yves. The baron leaned over the railing and listened as Thomas explained the danger to the lady. Lord Yves then called out to Lord de Umfraville.

"My lord, I would like you and your daughter to celebrate with us at the feast this evening. I am certain there are matters to discuss amongst you and Sir Thomas and I offer my services to mediate any...difficulties."

Annora's father opened his mouth to argue with the powerful lord and would have until Yves nodded to his steward, who would do his bidding, and to his commander, who very ably kept the peace during this huge gathering. Soon, a group of guards surrounded the man, giving him no choice but to comply.

"Since I must be present for the upcoming challenge, I bid you return to the keep with my men. You will be given chambers and a chance to eat and refresh yourselves." He leaned closer to his steward then and whispered some words, glancing at Annora as he did. "My lady, I am certain this day's events have proven exhausting to you. I beg you to accept my hospitality until arrangements are finalized." Her gaze met his, and, for the first time today, he saw her smile at the word *arrangements*.

"I thank you for your consideration, my lord. 'Twould be my pleasure."

With Annora safe, the tension melted from him and the bone-deep exhaustion and pain from the injuries he'd received flooded in. Martel urged him to return to his tent and see to his wounds, and Thomas obeyed without argument. There would time to see her at the feast, and then, when the melee was done and the documents ready to be signed, he would finally be able to begin his life...again.

Annora stood in the silence of the large, well-lit chamber and waited for her heart to stop racing. The noblewoman who'd brought her to this room had introduced herself as a particular friend of the baron's and one he'd asked to see to her comfort. Annora suspected she understood what kind of a friend this woman was to the powerful man—the very same kind Annora would soon be to Thomas—but how could she feel anything but relief and gratitude in this moment?

Thomas had understood her message and what her father had planned for her and warned the baron. Her father must be waiting elsewhere in the keep, for he had boldly yelled out that he would not leave without her.

What would he do now? Did he face ruin, having lost their lands and claim to Prudhoe Castle? Would William take the lands after hungering for so long for their return from the English kings? How would her father pay le Govic's fee if he had no lands from which to draw the gold needed? If she were no longer in his control, what price would le Govic demand?

For the first hours here, all she accomplished was bathing and eating at her leisure and dressing only when

Margaret arrived, having been summoned to the keep with instructions on what to bring. Then, while waiting for the challenge to the death of the tournament to conclude, God rest the loser's soul, she had time to think about what was to come. Well, she wondered about what was to come.

The fear that had lived within her, coiled deep and waiting to explode, had eased. Knowing more about what Thomas would expect of her after their time together, Annora knew it would be pleasurable and not the life of terror that the other outcome would have meant. She would go with him, live with him, share his bed and spend her life in his arms until...

She pushed that away again, as she had each time it reared up in her thoughts. She must speak with him, plainly and forthrightly, to find out how this would work between them. Did he have a place to live? A manor home or keep on the lands he would regain from the king? Or did he plan to build one? Would he allow her to bring Margaret with her, so the young woman did not face her father's wrath at his failure? Would she function as chatelaine as she'd been raised to do, or only occupy his bed and those other places he'd mentioned to her? So many things to discuss and sort through.

Margaret urged her to rest, for the feast would go long into the night, so Annora took advantage of the plush, feather-filled mattress and well-strung bed and fell deeply asleep. When her maid woke her, it was time to go below and celebrate the day's winners and commiserate with the losers, though in her situation, she suspected she would not do so.

Though Thomas was seated at the baron's table and many cups were raised in honor of his victory on the field, she was unable to speak to him for any longer than a moment or two. The baron took his self-appointed role as her protector seriously and made certain no one got too close to her for very long. Her own father was escorted to and from the table by guards who stood by awaiting any orders from their lord.

Then, before she knew it, she found herself back in the chamber and tended to by Margaret. In usual circumstances, she would feel aggrieved over the heavy-handed custody, but when she thought about what her fate could have been this day, she was grateful for such attention.

But she wanted Thomas. She wanted to see him and to talk to him about the fight. And to examine him for new injuries and to observe the condition of the older ones. She wanted...to touch him and to hold his flesh in her hands unimpeded by her garments or his. She wanted to find satisfaction in his embrace and be possessed by him.

She wanted. She wanted so much. And now, there was a possibility that she might get much of what, and who, she wanted. When, in the dark of night, the knock came at her door, her heart leapt with joy as she slid from the bed and made her way to open it.

There he stood in the shadowed corridor outside the chamber.

The man she loved.

And the baron.

Thomas had nearly come to blows with his host over seeing Annora. He almost regretted asking Lord Yves to protect her, not realizing it meant that he would be prevented from seeing her, too. Now, the only way to get to Annora was with the baron. Here they stood, outside the chamber, high in the baron's private tower, waiting for Annora to answer the door. When she did, he began to enter until the baron eased his way in first and blocked Thomas from crossing the threshold.

"I would speak with the lady first," the baron said before shutting the door in his face.

Thomas kept repeating in his thoughts that he should be grateful to the enigmatic lord for his help. It worked to distract him for several minutes, and then Thomas started pacing. How long could he speak with her? What did he need to ask her? Or tell her? Was she frightened? Did she have questions? Would she laugh for him again? What would she think when he spoke of...

The door opened, and Thomas rushed to it. The baron came out and closed the door behind him, motioning for him to wait. They walked a few paces down the hallway and stopped.

Keeping his voice lowered due to the lateness of the hour, Lord Yves explained, "The lady has told me that you two have an understanding, though she has not explained that or given me details," he said. Thomas opened his mouth to say something when the baron shook his head. "Truly, though curious, 'tis not my place to become involved any further in this matter. The important thing is the lady has given me assurances that you are not a danger to her and may visit her now." Lord Yves crossed his arms over his chest and tilted his head. "If you truly wish to visit her?"

Thomas heard the question being asked of him and wondered at it. As he turned to go to her chamber, Lord Yves stopped him again. And before he spoke, his demeanor changed—from a welcoming host to some kind of predatory being.

"I have heard elsewhere what your *arrangement* with the lady is and wonder at it."

"My lord?"

"I have heard rumors that you do not offer marriage to her. That you have already taken her virtue. And now you offer her a place as your leman and not your wife?"

He met the baron's gaze and felt as if some creature were judging him, able to discern the truth and apply the punishment if he were found wanting. How had the baron discovered those truths? Who knew and would have warned him so? Well, the man ran an efficient household and no doubt had spies everywhere to report back to him. None of that mattered for his intentions had changed and changed drastically.

"I will offer her marriage before we return to speak to King William." There. Would that satisfy him?

"Ah, so now you come to your senses?"

"I would like to think I am somewhat intelligent, my lord. Even if some of my behavior these last years speaks otherwise." Thomas rubbed his hands up through his very short hair and then shrugged. "How could I not see the value of the woman in that chamber? How could I want for anyone else after knowing her?"

"So, you will formalize your betrothal before leaving here? I can offer my clerk's services in drawing up the documents."

"Are you a marriage broker, my lord? Guaranteed a fee in negotiating this for the lady?" Thomas studied the man's face, for he'd paid little attention to his host before. "What is your interest here? Do you play some larger game with my liege lord and your own?" Rumors had flown all week about Lord Yves's loyalties and the presence of a large number of allies of the wayward prince at the tournament. Gatherings in the shadows. Alliances forming. Conspiracies abounding.

"Nay, none of that, Sir Thomas. In fact, I simply do not wish to find myself in the role of procurer when the one being bought is a young innocent without someone to advocate for her." A shadow flickered across the man's eyes then, as though a memory of someone moved within his thoughts.

"Just so, my lord." He was actually grateful for the man's intervention on Annora's behalf. If Thomas had not already changed his mind about marriage, mayhap the man's words and warnings would have steered him in that direction?

"Then I bid you a good night," the baron said with a nod. "Oh, just one more word," he added. "Have a care not to be seen here and worsen the gossip that swirls already." He turned away from Thomas and then back. The baron's gaze narrowed as he stared and then he spoke. "Do not think to cross me in this."

"Cross you?" Thomas frowned at the man. "How and why would I do such a thing?"

"If you do not offer marriage, I have decided you will answer to me. And if we meet on a field of honor, you will find me a worthier opponent than your last one."

With that, the mysterious baron of Rose Citadel walked away, leaving Thomas to ponder the words, and threats, he'd just heard. Once the sound of the man's footsteps was no longer echoing down the corridor, Thomas walked to Annora's door and eased it open.

She lay curled up on the large bed, looking very small in the middle of it. Only her soft, even breaths broke the silence. He smiled as he realized she'd fallen asleep while the baron had taken the time to chastise him outside.

He knew he should leave her be, but he just wanted to hold her in his arms and make sure this was real. That she would be his. Taking care not to disturb her, Thomas climbed slowly up on the bed, listening as the ropes creaked under his weight until he reached her. Sliding down onto his side, he eased her back into his arms.

"Thomas?" she whispered, her eyelashes fluttering as she tried to wake. "You are here."

"Hush now, sweetling. Go back to sleep," he said, kissing her hair and laying his arm over her to hold her close.

"Do not leave me," she murmured, already asleep.

So, he did not.

But the first rays of the dawn's sun woke him a few hours later, and he knew he must not be seen in her chambers. Thomas managed somehow to get out of the bed and the chamber without making noise enough to rouse her.

Only as he released the latch on the door and turned around did he realize his failure to leave unseen, for there stood Lord Yves with Annora's father. The baron blocked Lord de Umfraville from going farther in the hallway, but that did not stop the man from calling out his accusations. And demands. And naming his own daughter a harlot in this affair.

By the time the melee had begun, word had spread wide and far afield about Annora's shame and his own part in it. Though everyone involved in this had never confirmed that a marriage would result, everyone who heard that she was part of the prize assumed it would be the result. His plan at the beginning was that saying nothing about it would let everyone unimportant in this scheme to live in their false assumptions long enough for him to return to the king and sort things out.

She'd asked him not to humiliate her and before she was even aware of it, he had. Though many couples anticipated their vows, in an affair such as theirs that involved the matters of kings, he would have expected to marry first then bed his wife. Now, the marriage he'd decided to offer would look like a hasty decision *to her*, one forced on him rather than the choice he'd made, and she would leave here never certain of his words or promises.

Thomas felt bad about that. But come the feast, his public proposal would go far in alleviating any embarrassment. And once they left here, they need never see any of these people again. Believing all would soon be well, Thomas skirted the field where the melee was in progress and made his way to his tent, where he found Martel and Geoffrey organizing his belongings to begin packing.

When Martel held out a packet to him bearing the royal seal of Scotland, Thomas's stomach began to churn. After breaking the seal and reading the contents, Thomas called for his horse and rode up into the hills, away from everyone, away from the crowds and the gawkers and those complicit in this swirling drama that unfolded around him and pulled him to its center.

By the time Thomas returned to the encampment, he could tell from Martel's irritating smirk that the man knew what the message had directed him to do.

"Speak a word, and you will be digging your teeth out of the back of your throat. I swear it, Martel."

Wisely, the man bowed and sought out his own tent. It would not have helped anything, but Thomas really wished the man had spoken. He needed to punch something or someone right now. To strike out and release his anger. He remained inside until the dark of night began to fall, and then he made his way to the castle and inside to the keep. He knew what he must do.

To reclaim all his family had lost—the lands in Kelso, the keep and the farms, their centuries' old title of nobility and the wealth from those lands—all he had to do was give Annora up.

Nay, not give her up. Turn her away.

Expose her fall from honor, blame it her on actions and publicly repudiate her for it.

Shame her and, by doing that before all those attending the tournament, shame her father.

Part of the king's long-awaited, long-planned revenge for some personal insult offered years ago during the siege of Prudhoe by Annora's father, now coming back to be paid by her.

And Thomas was the instrument of that revenge, empowered to destroyed Annora's life in order to regain his.

The king expected him to carry out the orders.

Thomas had orchestrated this without ever realizing that he *was* the king's puppet, and he *was* being manipulated into setting this all in motion. Now, the puppet master twisted the strings for his own purposes, for his own needs, and the hell with everyone used and discarded.

He'd sworn to do anything the king asked of him when he had nothing to lose from it. He would have agreed to most anything that day when given a taste of the light after months of darkness. He'd put his needs above anyone else's when the king beckoned him from the dungeon.

He was more than willing to pay a price for his freedom, but did it have to be her?

Nineteen

Annora grew more nervous by the moment.

Something had happened this morn, and she did not know the whole of it yet. Now sitting in the baron's solar awaiting his arrival, she could not enjoy the delicacies offered to her nor the special wines he provided to his honored guests. Her stomach ached, and her head throbbed.

Though she was not alone, very few approached or addressed her, leaving her sitting in a large chair in one corner of the large chamber. Her reputation now lay in shreds as word of her shame in giving herself to Thomas before he'd earned the right to claim spread through the keep and town and people. So, it did not surprise her that others stood aside from her. The chill in the summer evening's air was warmed by the large hearth near her, but it did not ease the growing cold within her.

And still, they waited. Just when she'd reached the end of her patience, the door opened, and four men entered. None of them were happy. None of them wanted to be near the others, for once inside the chamber, they separated and walked as far from each other as they could.

Thomas came towards her. His servant stopped and

stood by the door. Her father walked to the table where the wine was and poured himself a full cup. And their host strode to the other end of the room and spoke with his steward, who left quickly. Annora watched the movements and was struck by how they each shifted as though on some game board of chance. When Thomas crouched down before her and took hold of her hand, she shivered in fear.

"I am sorry, Annora," he whispered. "Sorrier than I can say, sweetling."

Before she could ask for an explanation, he released her hand and stood, glaring at his servant by the door. He changed then, from the warm, generous lover back to the rogue who she'd met first. One who sought only his own pleasure.

"Do you wish to begin, Sir Thomas?" Lord Yves asked.

"Damn him!" her father called out before swallowing several mouthfuls of the wine in his cup. She'd seen her father angry, but this was different. He was unnerved. "You have broken our agreement. You have shamed my honor by taking my daughter's virtue when it was not yours to take and without an offer of marriage!"

"You and others may have *expected* marriage to result from all of this, Lord de Umfraville, but the agreement you signed did not specify that," Thomas said in a voice so cold she expected to feel its chill on her skin. "I came here to seduce your daughter, and that I did," he paused then but did not bother to look at her. The gasps echoed through the large chamber as she felt shame burn her cheeks. "But my intention was never marriage...to her."

Whispered gasps filled the chamber as all their gazes turned on her. She slid her hands down onto the arms of the chair and clenched them to keep from screaming. Lord Yves straightened up and took two paces towards Thomas before one of the other men stopped him.

"You do admit taking her to your bed? To dishonoring her? Insulting me?" her father asked.

"I admit to taking her to my bed, and you deserved to be insulted, but I did not dishonor her. I came here seeking the king's favor and the return of all I'd lost. I paid the price he asked but today, I discovered that the final cost would be her shame. For my sins and for yours, Lord de Umfraville. *She* was expected to pay her all."

Thomas walked to her and crouched down once again. She tried to look everywhere and nowhere but especially not at him until he took her chin and gently turned her head so had to see him. The tears filled her eyes, then overflowed down her cheeks.

"I did not dishonor her because she offered to me that most precious part of herself," he said. "She was in the worst situation a woman could face and she faced it with grace and intelligence and a sense of honor that shamed me into realizing the truth of my life."

"Thomas." His name was uttered by his servant like the warning growl of a wild animal. "Do not do this."

Her chest felt ready to burst from holding her breath for so long. When Thomas stood quickly and strode to her father, she let it all out in a gasp. Reaching out, he grabbed her father by his garments and pulled him closer.

"I know not what sin you committed against the king, but she will not bear it for you."

"What?" her father asked as he tried to loosen Thomas's grasp.

"You go to the king, who now holds claim to Prudhoe Castle, and sort this mess out. You have committed some grievance against him, my lord. You should bear the cost of your own sins." He shook her father before dropping him to the floor.

The servant walked over to Thomas then. "Are you certain this is what you wish to do? You know what you will lose."

"This," Thomas said, motioning with his hand to

indicate the group of them, "was not my arrangement with the king, Martel. And you know it because you drew it up yourself." Thomas looked at her then. "The king wanted me to win Prudhoe for him by challenging your father in a way he could not refuse. I did that, but without knowing the larger scheme around us, or that he would change the parameters and force a price that I am not willing to pay." He came to her and lifted one of her hands to his mouth and kissed it. Warmth returned to the place where his mouth touched.

"Some game played between the highest and the mightiest of the lands I suspect, Lord Yves." Thomas turned to face their host. The baron's smile in reply was not reassuring nor one she would want to see again. He was clearly more involved with this intrigue than he would admit. "Now, I am done with it. I carried out my part and am finished but for one matter."

He knelt then before her and took both of her hands in his. Her heart, which had been tearing itself apart, now became whole as he whispered to her the words that she'd never expected to hear.

"Be my wife, Annora? I have little to offer you, less than when this misadventure began, but I offer it to you."

"Thomas, are you sure? You will lose everything you suffered for and could gain back."

"Nay, I lost everything through my dishonorable actions and am not certain I deserve their return. You know, when I thought I might lose to le Govic, I did not think of the title or land. I thought of you. And the thought of losing you was too much to risk."

Annora felt hope flow back into her heart now and allowed herself to believe. She had offered him her body, and now he offered his heart to her. He had vanquished her enemy and saved her soul. And now he asked to share her life.

"Aye, I will," she whispered back.

"Come now," Lord Yves called out as his servants opened the door and began ushering those within towards the Great Hall. "A feast, a celebration awaits us there."

Within a few minutes, they were alone in the solar.

"You may want to wait until I sort this out with the king." Drawing her up to her feet, Thomas sat down behind her and pulled her onto his lap.

"Are you changing your mind already?"

"Nay, my lady, but you might want to consider if you want this arrangement when you think about what you get out of it."

"I think we need a new agreement between us," she said, enjoying the feel of his body so close to hers. She shimmied a bit, and he groaned.

"And what would this new agreement say?" He tugged the veil out of his way, moved her braid and kissed the back of her neck, sending spirals of pleasure shooting through her body.

"I will have you anytime I want you, anywhere I want you, and in any manner I say. And you will allow me to touch you however I want to and in any manner," she said, her voice growing deeper as the thought of what she wanted to do, and how she wanted to touch him, crossed her mind.

"You still have no idea of what that all entails, do you, sweetling?" She turned to meet his gaze and shook her head.

"Nay, Thomas. But I am certain you can help me find my way."

He laughed then, a sound she only recently thought she would never hear again. It filled her with warmth and need.

And love.

He filled her with love.

The rest would have to work itself out.

Epilogue

Almost a year later
Kelso, The Borders of Scotland

"Come with me!" she said, tugging his hand to make him follow.

She made her way slowly these days as her belly grew larger. If the midwife were correct, the bairn, as they called babies here in Scotland, would arrive around midsummer's day. That seemed fitting, since they'd met at a midsummer's tournament and joined their lives in a way she'd never thought possible.

Now, in the late afternoon, the sun was still high enough in the sky to provide them with several more hours of daylight. And she had a plan for how they could spend it.

"Have a care, Annora," he urged. "'Tis slippery here. What has you rushing so?"

"I found a place I want you to see," she said.

He'd mentioned it to her long ago, once more after that first time. Mayhap on their way to see the king in Edinburgh or mayhap on their way here after the king relented and allowed Thomas to keep what he'd been promised? Once the king realized that her father had been insulted and humiliated by all that had transpired, he accepted Thomas's explanation...and the new wife he presented as well. Annora had tucked this bit of knowledge away as she had many others, for the time when she would need it.

Or rather, need him.

Now, joining with him was more difficult, but that had not diminished her desire for him. Though he was considerate as he'd always been and made no demands on her, she tired of waiting for him to make the first step. She smiled, wondering what his reaction would be when he saw this place. They rounded the last curve on the path, and she stopped.

The nearby river turned just yards away, leaving a pool of water collecting here. She'd checked it and found she could walk into it easily and could stand in it, for there was no current to push her about. And, with the way the sunlight shone on it all day, the water was warmer than the rest of the river flowing there.

"You spoke once of a place such as this where you would take me in the water, over and over again," she said softly. When he pressed against her, his erect cock did not surprise her. It never did. Annora leaned back and rested her head on his chest, knowing he would let his hands wander over her body.

"I want you here, my love. I want you in the water. I want you over and over. And then I want to lie on the bank there with you and let the breezes dry our skin."

He cleared his throat several times before forcing a word, any word, out.

"Have I told you how much I love the way you seduce me, sweetling?" He gathered her gown and kirtle up in his hands and pulled them off in one motion, leaving her naked but for her hose and shoes. "Have I told you how much I love you?"

"You may have, but you can tell me again once we are in the water."

Just a short while later, he did, and she did, and they did.

And their son was born a fortnight later on midsummer's day, as was fitting.

Across A Windswept Isle

Ailis lost the love of her life… or is he standing right in front of her?

Lachlan MacLean loved his enemy's daughter, but duty called for him to marry another. Attacked by an unseen assailant and left to die in a fiery grave, he survived and now wanders the isle of Mull without any memory of his past. He seeks anyone who might know him but the one he wishes to find is the woman who haunts his dreams and visions. When he encounters her, she is being given in marriage to another man. He doesn't know her name, but he knows he must have her to regain his life.

Ailis MacKinnon lost the love of her life in a terrible fire and months later is being forced by her father to marry. When she refuses and is given to the next man who enters the keep instead, she discovers that the mysterious 'Iain' reminds her of the man she lost. Worse, he encourages her to be the woman she should be. As the battle of wills between father and daughter builds, so does the passion between her and this hooded man.

Will she be able to claim the man she lost knowing that exposing his identity brings danger back to him? Or can she give him up now that she has found him?

Prologue

Aros Castle, Isle of Mull
September, In the Year of Our Lord 1490

Death stalked a slow path through the village and keep of the Clan MacLean on the Isle of Mull. It took the young and the old, the weak and the strong, and the rich and the poor. It cared not if a life had been well- or ill-lived. It took and took until, satiated, it left as silently as it had arrived. Clan MacLean mourned the deaths of so many of its own.

Lachlan MacLean surveyed the number of graves before him with a bit of shock and sadness. His mother and brother lay beneath a newly-strewn covering of dirt at his feet. His father, devastated in a way Lachlan had never seen, stared off into the misty hills that led away from their village. Lachlan swore that Dougal MacLean aged a score of years in just this last fortnight.

Villagers, kith and kin drifted away after the priest finished his blessing. Lachlan turned to go. The rough hold stopped him.

"Her father comes on the morrow. We will discuss the matter when he does." His father nodded across the graves to tall, lithe Wynda MacLeod, his late brother's betrothed.

He'd completely forgotten about the young woman in the hurried arrangements for the many burials. Now, Lachlan noted that her calm, blue eyes stared over at the keep, unfocused as though in deep contemplation. When her eyes shifted and met his, the lack of grief in hers surprised him.

"The matter?" The older man now clenched his arm harder and shook him. "Father, I canna …"

"Ye will do yer duty now that ye are my heir."

With those words, his father released him and strode to the keep, not glancing back at his living son, or the dead one, again. Lachlan understood the message and the warning in his father's words. Everything had changed on the death of his brother.

He must get word to Ailis before she heard it from someone else.

Ailis MacKinnon believed they would marry. He had pledged his heart and honor to her. They had plans and had promised their lives to each other. They hoped that their fathers would eventually agree as a way to keep the peace, though neither would like the idea of linking their families. The MacKinnons were a thorn in the side of the MacLeans of Mull and had been for generations, so he and Ailis had made certain that few knew the true extent of their relationship.

If his father wished to broker a marriage between his second son, and now heir, and The MacLeod's daughter, Lachlan would be expected to disavow his promises to Ailis. If word got out that he'd broken faith with her, the tenuous peace between their families would shatter and make their clans enemies.

But none of that was the worst thing about this. The worst was that he would be forced to marry another and break Ailis' heart.

Lachlan went into the keep and climbed the stone steps into the tower to his own chamber. He found some parchment and wrote the message that would bring her to their trysting place.

He'd just handed it to a boy to take to her when Artair stepped in front of him.

"Do ye think that is a good idea?" he asked, looking in the direction the servant had gone. Artair knew how they communicated secretly … and where they met.

"She must hear it from me."

"So, 'tis a deal already done?" Artair asked.

"The MacLeod comes on the morrow to make the arrangements. Father has decided that I will take my brother's place and marry the MacLeod lass."

"Wynda." So much anger infused the one word. Lachlan looked closely at his closest friend.

"Have ye knowledge of the woman that I dinna have?" At his friend's silence, he narrowed his gaze and asked again. "Is there aught I should ken, Artair?"

"She had no liking for yer brother," he muttered.

"It matters not, the betrothal was made and she agreed. As will this next one."

"Aye, it matters not," Artair repeated. "Ye are the heir now."

Lachlan couldn't understand why his friend's words, nay the tone of his words, bothered him. Something swirled in the back of his thoughts, glimpses of gestures and looks exchanged between his friend and his brother's betrothed. The truth struck him. He gasped at the recognition of it.

"I would never betray ye, Lachlan. 'Tis done as of this moment."

Artair held out his hand, offering his word and solemn vow that he wouldn't betray his trust and consort with the woman Lachlan would marry. Lachlan paused before accepting his friend's hand. Artair was a man of his word. Artair was one of few men Lachlan would trust and had trusted with his life and safety.

"I ken," he said, clasping the man's forearm with his hand. After a few seconds, he released his hold and stepped back.

"When will ye see *her*?" Artair asked as they walked out of the keep and into the yard. Not many knew of the extent of his involvement with Ailis. They kept it quiet because of the tenuous situation between their families.

"In the morn. Once The MacLeod is sighted, word will spread." Lachlan nodded to the stables. "I have matters to arrange."

As he walked away, Artair spoke his name. Lachlan turned and saw a strange expression on his friend's face.

"She is not as she appears, Lachlan. She never was."

Did his friend speak of Wynda or of Ailis? Did he know something more after all? Before he could ask for an explanation, Artair walked away.

The rest of the day passed in silence, his family still reeling from the deaths around them. Supper was a somber meal. Those living in the keep had little patience for idle or joyful chatter that night. Rest wouldn't come to him, so he rose long before dawn to be on his way.

He reached the cottage just as the sun broke the eastern horizon. There was no sign of Ailis, so he walked inside to wait. Smiling at the memories of this place and of her, Lachlan tugged open the wooden shutters to watch for her approach. When the sound of footsteps behind him interrupted his thoughts, he turned, thinking he'd missed her arrival.

"Lachlan," she said softly as he turned.

That was the last thing he would remember.

One

Dun Ara Castle, Isle of Mull
Eight months later

Ailis MacKinnon sat at the table on the dais, waiting for her father's words. From his ruddy face and the way he kept starting and stopping, he was angry. Davina threw furtive glances in her direction, as though asking for her help. Ailis snorted. Davina, her stepmother and former closest friend would rot in Hell before Ailis helped her.

"Ye're being willful, girl," her father shouted. "Ye will accept this man!"

Silence reigned over the entire hall as all gathered there waited for the next argument between the chieftain and his daughter. Ailis knew it. Her father prepared for it. Even Davina saw it coming. It was Davina's voice that gave her father pause.

"Husband," she said, rising and walking to his side. "Mayhap we should discuss this in the solar?" Davina placed her hand on Ailis' father's arm. He took a breath, clearly considering his wife's plea. For a moment, Ailis thought he might accept Davina's suggestion but he shook off her hand and stomped his foot.

"Nay, Wife," he said, "'tis too late for a private word on this matter."

Davina startled at the sharpness of his tone and stepped back. Ailis watched as he grabbed Davina's hand and tugged her closer to him. Tears burned in Ailis' eyes as she watched, yet again, as her father softened for … *her.*

Ailis wanted to run. She wanted to leave the table, leave the keep and even her father's lands. Everything in her life had fallen apart. There was no way to put the pieces back together. Her friend was happy. Her father was happy. She was desolate and no one seemed to notice or care.

"Ailis! Come here now!"

She'd not realized she'd turned away until his call turned her back towards him. Lord Duncan MacNeil stood at her father's side watching the drama unfold. As she walked around the table towards them, she saw neither anger nor any emotion on the old man's face. If he was insulted by her refusal, she cared not. Pushing her hair over her shoulders, she stopped before her father and curtsied.

She nodded at Lord Duncan, out of respect, truly. The poor man had no idea of what he'd agreed to in bringing his suit to her father. He likely believed his offer was a kind one for a noble born woman with such … deformities as she did. That thought made her tug the leather gloves higher onto her arms before she faced her father.

"Lord Duncan is of good standing with his chieftain and his king. A marriage like this will benefit ye. Ye will accept his offer of marriage."

Ailis felt the eyes of those gathered moving from one to another as they watched this disagreement continue. A glance past her father revealed Davina's concern. Ailis looked away from her.

"I fear I canna."

The simple statement sent everyone into chaos. Shouts and whispers filled the air around them until her father waved his hand and everyone quieted.

"Ye seem to think this is a request, Daughter. Mistake not

my resolve that ye will marry Lord Duncan."

Ailis felt a small trickle of sweat run down her face and another on her back. Defying her father wasn't an easy task, nor one she did lightly. But the thought of taking this man to husband when she had already promised herself to another was too hard, even if that man was now dead. Facing her father's bluster wasn't something she wished to do, even knowing he had promised her mother as she lay dying that he would never force their daughter to marry.

"Father," she began, lowering her head and her voice. "I canna and willna marry this man."

He reached out for her hands and realized his error before touching her. Instead, he lifted her chin with his finger to bring their gazes to meet.

"Ye must marry, Ailis. Ye will marry Lord Duncan."

"Nay."

Instead of the reaction she expected of her father, that of any irate man when faced with a recalcitrant and defiant daughter, the one she witnessed startled her. His gaze narrowed, he glanced from her to the man involved before huffing out a loud breath and walking to the table. Even Davina was surprised. She met Ailis' eyes and shrugged.

Her father grabbed a goblet and filled it from the pitcher sitting there. He drank it down and filled it again. Turning to face them, he swallowed the contents in several mouthfuls and slammed the cup on the table. She jumped, Davina jumped and the rest gasped.

"Ye willna marry Lord Duncan then?" She shook her head. "Fine." He walked to her and stared at her, his gaze softening for so short a time she thought she'd not seen it happen. "I have labored under a promise, sworn as all of ye ken, to my late, sainted wife not to force our daughter to marry against her will. A man of honor, I have upheld that promise."

"Father—" she began. Mayhap she had pushed him too far? Glancing at Lord Duncan, she wondered if she should relent.

"But even my beloved dead wife wouldna expect this behavior in her daughter."

Ailis gasped in shock and pain. Tears escaped before she could stop them. Her mother had passed before she had lost Lachlan. Her mother couldn't have known how this would be for her. Or how hard it would be to watch her friend betray her and marry her father, fresh from her mother's death. Now, 'twas clear that her father's regard for her mother and the vow made was at an end.

"My late wife would understand there has to be an end to this and a way to give ye into the care of a husband." She heard Davina's whispered pleas and saw her father brush her words off.

"I will give ye a choice, Ailis," her father said. "Consent to marry Lord Duncan now or ye will marry the man who next enters my keep."

She couldn't help herself. She looked to doors of the keep across the chamber. Closed because of the storm raging outside, 'twas almost as though everyone witnessing this expected the doors to crash open and a man to enter as if told beforehand to do so.

After that did not happen, she turned back to face her father. Certain that, if given time, she'd find a way to change his mind on this declaration, Ailis decided to agree with his demand. Aye, there would be time to allow her stepmother to soothe his temper as she seemed to in times like this one.

"I will marry the next man through the door, Father."

Meet Terri Brisbin

RWA RITA®-nominated, award-winning and *USA Today* best-selling author **Terri Brisbin** is a mom, a wife, grandmom(!) and a dental hygienist who has sold more than 3.5 million copies of her historical and paranormal romance novels and novellas in more than 25 countries and 20 languages. Her current and upcoming historical and paranormal/fantasy romances are published by Harlequin Historicals, Oliver Heber Books and independently, too.

Visit her website for more info about Terri, her works and upcoming events.

Connect with her on
Facebook @TerriBrisbinAuthor
X (Twitter) @Terri_Brisbin
Instagram @TerriBrisbin

TerriBrisbin.com

A Midsummer Knights Romance Series

A Tournament World of Chivalry, Intrigue, and Passion

Summer, 1193. England is in turmoil, and a great tournament is scheduled near the border of Scotland and England. The greatest knights and lords from England, Scotland, Ireland, and France have gathered to compete for a great prize. There will be celebrations and jousts and feasting. It will an exhibition of chivalry and warrior skills, a breeding ground for treason…and for love.

Forbidden Warrior by Kris Kennedy

The Highlander's Lady Knight by Madeline Martin

The Highlander's Dare by Eliza Knight

The Highland Knight's Revenge by Lori Ann Bailey

My Victorious Knight by Laurel O'Donnell

An Outlaw's Honor by Terri Brisbin

Never If Not Now by Madeline Hunter